BAPTIZER

AND 10 MORE ALABAMA NIGHTMARES

KEVIN LaPORTE

INVERSE

Table of Contents

For Mama.

For voicing pride in my endeavors, no matter how weird or alien to you. I miss you every day.

BAPTIZER

1

The Drowning of Falls City

Moving was just the worst. And moving twice in six months was plain torture. Melody Landover squatted in her newest room amongst cardboard skyscrapers not opened since she, her parents, and her big brother Mike forfeited their country home outside Falls City, Alabama that summer of 1961. The power company planned to flood half the county, and all the people there had to go. Daddy was a chicken seller for Pilgrim's Pride over in Cullman, but he took Alabama Power's payoff and dropped anchor forty-five minutes west in middle-of-nowhere Double Springs to be far from that pit of sin in Birmingham.

In Melody's lap was a dusty Easter hat box salvaged from her mother's trash some Spring past. One tooth-chipped thumbnail dug at its pink lid, pried it up with a little pop. She glanced side-eye at the closed door, just in case, and pulled the top away. Inside lay Daddy's kerchief she cried into at Mawmaw's funeral, all brown and emerald paisleys each coiling about the other along drafts of Old Spice. A pinch at the silky rag lifted it away from a purple mortarboard and golden tassel, Mama's graduation cap. Winston County High School. Class of 1941. Melody was just two years from depositing her own cap into this fragrant old time capsule, and she couldn't wait. Down beneath was a crumpled assortment of letters from Spanish pen pals, wish-you-were-here's from well-traveled cousins, and postcards from her Falls City youth group from their trip to the Holy Land that time when she had the mumps.

Sacred as they were, all those assembled treasures merely hid a forbidden relic of value greater than their sum. Delicately sleeved in assorted onion-skin papers in the basement of the hat box was a long-play vinyl record, glistening black and intricately grooved. The center label was peeled away to disguise its messages and the name of the voice that sang them, but Melody heard the stylings of Elvis Aaron Presley in her head even as she plied apart the album's bed sheets to take it in. This was the soundtrack to King Creole, her second copy of the King's 1958 masterpiece. Daddy melted the first in the fireplace after he found her singing along to Trouble on his turntable, the one reserved only for gospel hymns and, then, only on Sunday mornings before services.

Daddy, and the entirety of the Falls City Pentecostal Assembly, warred against the evils of rock and roll from its inception, and Elvis was at the head of the beast. His bluesy crooning, "Well, I'm evil, so don't you mess around with me," didn't soften their stance, and, in fact, hearing those lyrics fly from Melody's own mouth drove Daddy to seek counsel for her from their preacher, Brother Teddy. She walked there from school on Tuesdays and Thursdays for six whole months, enduring every contortion of scripture to somehow prove music not printed in hymnals was a fabrication of the Morningstar himself. Rock and roll, the eighth deadly sin. But, more than that, Brother Teddy pushed her to reject all worldly things and to seek salvation in the name of Jesus, whatever that gobbledygook meant. He wanted her to be baptized once she purified her life of all things fun. Music. Television. Boys. Raised Christian, Melody was not impervious to his guilt-laced tactics, despite the inane logic of them all.

She cried herself to sleep many a night after those sessions, mortally afraid these simple pleasures in a world of endless wars would surely earn her a permanent spot in the fires of Hell. Though, not completely unlike the delusional and – she now knew – ill-intended, musical notions of Brother Teddy, she subverted logic to believe an all-seeing God was somehow blind to a second King Creole record shielded from divine view by the loves and the losses emanating from its fellow inhabitants in the hat box.

Melody mock-traced the leader space for track four on the album, silently mouthing Trouble to herself.

"I'm only made out of flesh, blood and bone…"

She didn't have long before Mama called her for church, the latest congregation of awkward introductions and bless-your-heart's she endured for the sake of Christian inclusion since the Falls City kidnappings sent Brother Teddy to prison. Her vinyl secret fell silently back into its bed at the bottom of her memories, and she slipped the whole kit and caboodle into the deepest, darkest place under her latest bed.

The back seat of Daddy's Chrysler was extra lonely on church nights Mike played sick. On Wednesdays, WIXI AM out of Cullman played an hour of gospel music from 6:00 to 7:00 p.m., as everyone made their way to services, and Daddy commanded utter, respectful silence during The Blackwood Brothers' rendition of That's What Heaven Will Be and his favorite, The Davis Sisters' Rain in Jerusalem. Any words from Melody were allowed two-minute commercial windows before the inevitable, cutting shush. Although, on that night, the opening chords of a Statler Brothers standard sent his hand frantically for the knob, nudging the radio off with a reflexive wrist flick. He hated the Statler Brothers something fierce.

The ensuing silence birthed awkward topics. Daddy's head turned a quarter-rotation toward Mama.

"Don't you think it's time Melody was baptized?"

This again. Mama wrinkled her lip, glanced back at my widening eyes.

"Parker, the kidnappings were just last year. She's not ready. It can wait until…"

"Whoever believes and is baptized will be saved, but whoever does not believe will be condemned," he cut her off, "That's Mark 16:16. Still think it's something that can wait?"

Mama did not back down, and bless her for it.

"Don't you understand her fears? Brother Teddy took her friends in the night, drugged them, and baptized them against their will. If he wasn't caught, she might have been next on his list."

Daddy braked to an abrupt stop. Threw his arm over the bench seat and twisted to stare Melody down.

"I understand she needs to fear the Lord more than a servant gone astray. Follow the Word of God and be free of fear. First John 4:18 says, 'Perfect love casts out all fear.'"

He started the car moving again, flipped his gaze back to the road, bypassing Mama's incredulous furrows.

"Besides," he continued, "Brother Teddy is locked away for fifteen years, and the church where he took those kids will be gone tomorrow when the power company floods the old town for the hydroelectric plant. We should go watch and get some closure. I'll take the day."

In other words, Melody enjoyed a respite from baptism equal to the time it took the new lake to submerge the scene of the crimes, but the sanctified dunking would follow soon after, regardless her voice in the matter. She wondered at the callous ignorance of it all right up to the driveway of the new church.

As gentlemen do, Daddy dropped her and Mama off at the foyer to the church sanctuary and parked the car. What followed was the same exact sequence of fake smiles and absent, nodding acknowledgements programmed to occur twice on Sunday and once on Wednesday for every week of Melody's life. The same three hairstyles over the same pallid faces spewing the same sad dogma. But Melody played her part. Keep chin up. Keep eyes forward. Keep quiet.

The familiar warble of How Great Thou Art from the organist's fingertips informed the assembled collective unconscious that it was time to take seats, and Daddy walked in. Either a half-inning of the evening's Yankees game or a quarter-cigarette filled the interim between parking space and grand entrance, no doubt. He deftly dropped in beside Mama in their freshly staked protectorate six pews back on the left edge of the right row. It was just polite to let the established squatters take their places first, and Mama did just that before making a claim.

Without cue, the well-trained mass spontaneously, obediently broke into harmonized lyrics of the song, that haunting phenomenon of disparate tones and vocal acumen that inflated church walls and the mass hallucinations within them. Daddy couldn't remember the words, fumbled at a hymnal with one hand and for his spectacles in his vest pocket with the other. He was mortified, leaned into Melody with a warm, aftershave whisper.

"Honey, run out to the car and grab my specs, will ya?"

Melody was paroled. Her heartbeat skipped as though dropped from a rusty viaduct into the Black Warrior. She accepted the keys to the car and to her brief freedom.

Daddy's glasses stared from the dash as she approached, ignoring the white milk truck she noticed parked too close to the passenger-side door. Daddy better not see that. Who drove that thing to services, anyway?

Melody slipped into the driver's seat beneath a smirk of pretend power. Left hand on the wheel, the other slid the key into the switch with an agility that conjured cigarettes and James Dean. A cool half-turn forward, and the juice lit the radio. She worked her best nonchalance, no-look turned the AM dial from WIXI's 1480 down to 960. WBRC played rock and roll, and she twisted right into a sneak preview of Elvis' latest, Little Sister, that scandalous invitation to sin under guise of cautionary tale. Daddy wouldn't miss her for two more little minutes.

The bliss of new music sealed her eyes for moments beyond the song's end, but they fluttered open at a motion outside the windshield. She was caught.

"Daddy," Melody started apologetically, but there was nobody. A chill crawled from fingertips through elbows, and her breath left her. Fear froze her face forward, even as her eyes rolled left. A pair of trousered legs over spit-shined oxfords reflected in the side mirror. He outraced her to the door controls, tore it open and shoved his rag-gloved right fingers into her screaming mouth, palm crushing her nostrils from above. Her head filled with the acrid-sweet vapor of something like nail polish remover, and she stopped screaming, stopped resisting, stopped everything.

Everybody dozed in church occasionally, but Melody awoke from her nightmare fully fetal on the pew, prayer hands tucked tight between her knees. No chance Mama let her get away with that. Where were her parents? The terror of knowing shut her eyelids right down, but her ears overcompensated to the point of panic. Soft sobs surrounded her. And a grown man repeatedly grunted to clear his throat, a hint of his voice in those guttural utterances. Him. Realization brought hot tears. Brother Teddy.

She forced her eyes into taut, draining slits, lifted herself to look over the next pew and almost rolled to the floor. Her arms were bound at the wrist with chord wrapped back again around her knees into a fat knot behind. Hog-tied.

Spectral daylight diffused through stained glass and the wet of her eyes. Did he hold hostage the entire congregation through the night? No, the truth came with recognition of the haloed Gabriel watching indifferently from the glass above her. She was in the old church in Falls City, and today was the day of the flood.

The clearing throat gave way to praying murmurs in that emphatic, whispered cadence reserved by Brother Teddy and others of his ilk for the end-of-service salvation of souls. As though God only acted on the requests of those who implored him like a dog that kept knocking over the trash. There were resigned protestations from unseen others as the prayers advanced on Melody's place in the sanctuary. In that half-silence, another sound like rain came clear, a gentle water noise rising against the side of the building. Melody pulled uselessly at her knots, snorted in despair.

Brother Teddy popped up from the pew ahead of her, his face wrapped in a leather mask fashioned from a zippered bible cover, the big kind purchased from door-to-door salesmen and gilded with the family name. The cowl was cut so its golden cross angled diagonally down from left to right, weaponized into an arrow aimed at her soul. His blue left iris was barely visible through the one hole carved from the thing. It took her in, dilated and contracted madly, the hungry mouth of a monster. He stepped onto the seat to tower over, leaned in with cupped and beaten hands.

"Bless you, Melody."

That whisper again, emphasis on all the wrong syllables.

"For you have sinned. The lust of youth, for men and for music by men and not of our Lord. It's not your fault, girl."

"Brother Teddy, please," she pled. An uninterrupted forefinger rose to shush her.

"Fret not, for today, we wash it all away in waves of salvation, baptized and cleansed of sin for all time by the living water of Jesus."

The water lapped at the stained glass, and Brother Teddy noticed.

"Come now. Join us," he said, easily lifted her with one arm and carried her into the front pew, where five others lay at intervals. He dropped her facing the altar, where three more dangled upside down, each tied to inverted crosses left from the Easter pageant, their heads barely off the floor. Frantic eye contact among them all conjured no speech, every one afraid to draw attention. This web of quiet betrayed the pounding at the windows, and they throbbed under the pressure.

Brother Teddy knelt before the crucified, brushing each forehead in time with head-thrusting rises in the volume of his muttered prayers. Melody recognized all three. Dick Phillips got a car before anyone else in their class. He didn't even have a license yet. Landon McCord was a bullied poor boy from a dirt road community, always just as scared as he was right then. Shelly Baxter called every girl with nicer clothes than her a whore, so she said it a lot. But none of them deserved the common bond they were about to share.

Rivulets of water snuck under the doors, beneath the pews and into sight. Brother Teddy tested the spongy carpet with skeptical fingers. The zipper-edged mask seemed to grin. By the time he stood and stepped back, the oxfords positively splashed into the edge of the flood. His arms went skyward, and he danced the dance of a two-year-old in a mud puddle, knees high and fast, kicking up high, joyous arcs.

The water cleared his ankles, and he cupped two handfuls, sloshed it onto Dick's face.

"In the name of the Father," Brother Teddy blurted, "And his Son!"

Another aimed splash, this one onto the craning, hyperventilating noggin of Landon McCord, then a wet, almost playful slap at the rushing waters toward a flinching Shelly.

"And the Holy Spirit! I consecrate this rising tide. May it lift us from this Earthly plane and filter from us the wrongs we perpetrated against the Word of God Almighty!"

The first window burst beneath the now-holy water's onslaught, and Brother Teddy jerked in startled reflex before gathering himself once more in the face of the torrent. He laughed nervously, embarrassed at his reaction. Melody wept silently, hopeless yet transfixed in her knots. The crucified gurgled as the depths overtook their noses and mouths. They thrashed for maybe a minute before Landon fell limp.

Brother Teddy approached him, grasped high on his cross and spun him upright on a pin between the cross and its stand. Landon's neck lolled lifelessly in that rotation, and water spilled from ears, nose, and mouth. Brother Teddy baptized himself in these last streams of Landon's life, a labile tongue lapping thirstily at the drops under the mask's zipper track.

He cackled, "Draw water joyfully from the springs of salvation," and madly rubbed the wet into his mask face. He repeated the ritual with Dick and then Shelly when they drowned, quoted random baptism scripture from the deepening knee-high waters.

Melody's face dampened when a second window opened to the flood, and the rise quickened. In seconds, her clothes were soaked, that soggy bottom feeling she remembered from skinny dipping with her panties and bra still on. At that final moment, she chuckled at her own lameness.

Brother Teddy waded down the front pew, lifted the tied and screaming in turn above his head and slammed them headfirst into the drink, death at his hands and blessing on his lips. But Melody hid no sins to cleanse and no harm to regret. She loved her family. She loved laughing. And she loved Elvis. And no lackey of an indifferent God would take from her such precious things she could take with her.

Melody pushed the air from her lungs in one smiling resignation, rolled into the roiling waters of Falls City, and drank deeply of their mercy.

BAPTIZER

2

The Atlantis Beneath Smith Lake

The mid-20th century saw the creeping advance of electrical power across rural America and, with it, the need for power sources. And, where no sources existed, men created them. Hydroelectric stations called for deep waters, and men dammed age-old rivers in the name of artificial reservoirs to meet their need. These new waters swallowed thousands of square miles and, with them, places once occupied by men. Forgotten cities. Abandoned towns. And all the domiciles and places of gathering within each.

The empty streets and structures of Falls City, Alabama, dropped beneath the waters of the old Black Warrior River in the year of Our Lord, 1961, victim of the birth of Lewis Smith Lake, so named for the energy mogul who signed off on the dam that switched over the Warrior's waters. Not there was much to Falls City before her denizens got their government directives to vacate, but she was home to a few precious souls over the decades.

The night of August 13, 1982, was moon-bare, Lady Luna just a slim crescent up high, but no clouds obscured the reflection that bounced again off the still waters. And in that blue-white glow, Winston County Sheriff's Deputy Floyd Weston first saw the sobbing, handcuffed fisherman whose actions summoned the search and rescue team at this late hour. The twelve-year veteran paused as he killed his truck's engine, taking in the scene. The fisherman, one Jake Weaver, slumped against a muddy tire of the responding officer's Plymouth Fury, yelling between tearful gasps, "He backslid! He backslid!" But nothing else.

The man radioed his son was lost to the lake waters, but there was blood and weapon evidence in the boat, enough to detain him. Deputy Mark Manchon met Floyd at his trunk as he popped it to start unloading SCUBA gear.

"They really putting us in the water under dark of night, Floyd? Is it worth the risk for a boy that's surely already dead out there?"

Floyd hoisted a pair of tanks without glancing toward his partner.

"You'd feel different if it was your boy out there, Mark. Kids hereabouts know how to swim. Might be treading water right damn now, for all we know."

Mark threw a tank strap over one shoulder, made for the boat launch, called back, "Only if he can swim short half his blood supply, 'cause that's about what's left in his daddy's Bass Tracker."

Floyd moved in slow motion by the quarantined two-seater on his way to the Sheriff's flotilla vessel. Mark did not exaggerate. The kid took a heavy plastic paddle to the head, judging by the sheer amount of crimson that lined the boat's waterproofed innards. The things folks perpetrate on their own children…

Ten minutes was the ride out to the spot Daddy Weaver pointed to as the last where he saw "Junior" before he "fell" overboard. Every other son in Winston and Walker Counties was a "Junior" in those days, by damn.

The spotlights betrayed nothing on the lake surface 'round there, so it was into the drink for Floyd, Mark, and the other two responding team members, Hank Parsons and Billy Gabbert, both expert divers with years of pulling corpses out of overturned trucks under bridges and trapped cars in bubbling culverts, just for example.

They used the old out-and-back search technique, dropping a hundred feet of rope off the side, with wrist loops at quarter intervals down the length. Mark was at the end, a reflective buoy tethered to his belt for tracking from the tender on the boat. Floyd was next up, with Hank and Billy above them, in that order.

In murky waters in the dead of night, the boat pilot, a young'un named Jered, was the tender to keep heading and distance, communicating with beats or tugs in one direction or the other and in defined sequences down the rope. Night searching was dangerous work, and mostly blind, even with lights.

One at a time, they splashed in from the side of the boat, the water still hot from the summer day, and took their loops. Jered pulled at the line's knot on its anchor to check it and flashed a thumbs up. Mark rose an inch or two from the water, then lunged forward and down, his glittering buoy dancing a jig in its orbit above him. The rest followed in turn, adjusting their descent as the rope pulled and gave.

Floyd saw nothing. The night and the silt hooded him. Nothing new. He kicked and crawled along the long-practiced trajectory on instinct, felt the pull ahead, as Mark hit his depth, and then behind, as he found his own.

They swam left first, until the tender's signal, two beats left and three right, then turned 180 degrees and retraced their arc until beginning anew, right of the starting point. Less than ten feet into this fresh territory, something brushed Floyd's extended right bicep, a soft, rubbery thud. He jabbed at the line with his looped hand to stop the team, grasped toward the mystery object with the other.

Anxious seconds passed beneath the hollow gulping sound of his own breaths from the respirator, and then it was there. Forefinger and thumb found it at once, a collapsible, cloth, maybe vinyl, thing. Strings wrapped about his probing digits. A shoe! But nothing in it except a seeping dread that its drowned occupant floated nearby. He shifted it to the loop hand and used it to tap the rope to start the swim again, and the team above him moved on in response.

But, below him, the line went slack. Mark was either ascending, swimming sloppily – and he was too good for that – or he left the rope. And just the thought was preposterous. Something was wrong. Floyd popped the line again to stop the guys above. Before he could do anything, the tender sent down two right beats.

"Keep moving."

Annoyed from anxious uncertainty, Floyd reached with his free right hand and tugged four times a little too hard on the tether. The distress signal. The tender and other divers would hold position until he signaled again. He let loose the shoe, slipped his left hand from the loop, used it to form a clasp around the line, a guide as he descended its length toward the space where Mark used to be.

He glided elegantly through the murk for a man so petrified by what he might find at his destination, and the vacant end loop found his hand far quicker than he hoped. He groped about for a moment, as though Mark might be nearby, perhaps perpetrating some ill-conceived graveyard joke, but there was nothing.

Then, as he gripped the line for the three tugs that would signal to abort and pull up, he glimpsed light down and away, the only luminescence he sensed since dropping in. But, how? The deeper, the darker. That was just physics, right? Heavier sediment and further from the sun. Hell, he couldn't see his own dive light dangling from his wrist before his face. He closed his eyes to shake the illusion, but it was there again when he opened.

It had to be Mark. Disoriented or distressed or both and floundering down there, not knowing which way was up. Floyd had to move before Mark's light left his range of vision. His second set of four tugs on the rope signaled for help, and he kicked with conviction toward the inexplicable will o' the wisp that lured him.

Less than thirty feet on, and just twelve feet down, one strong pull of his arms drew him out of the dark and into clear waters, a translucent expanse that replaced his gulping breath sounds with a throbbing heartbeat. All the local in-jokes and folklore were true.

Before him, Floyd beheld Mayberry come Atlantis, 1950's Americana preserved in an aquarium. The boulevards of Falls City awaited, and the stained glass of the old First Baptist glowed bright from within. Floyd tried to convince himself that the church bells suddenly ringing midnight in his ears were a figment of the tall tales shared between boys at Royal Rangers campfires extinguished decades past.

Mark discovered this same spectacle, felt this same wonder, heard this same hymn that summoned the lost to the found. He was in that church, and Floyd bore nary a doubt about it. His eyes turned up at the black void above him now. The others would be along to help, but he couldn't wait. Oxygen was finite down here, but the list of things that could wrong was not.

The skeletal frames of Falls City clarified as he kicked into town, their fractures and dislocations vivid in proximity of his light. He swam at the second story, above the open-air post office and barber shop but past the tack and leather room atop the feed store. Their contents and occupants long washed away, these places yawned their death grimaces from every angle, their contorted window-and-door-frame faces surely brick-and-mortar facsimiles of their long-gone tenants.

The bells grew louder, and the church loomed just past the corner gas station. The sanctuary roof was intact compared to the rest of Falls City. Floyd couldn't find an opening to slip through, or even to scan the scene within. He swam down to a shattered window, only a neon blue shard of stained glass supported the hovering halo that remained of a devotee's handiwork atop the frame. His heartbeat and the bells clanged a percussive symphony then.

Grasping the inside edges of the window with each hand, deftly avoiding edged glass, Floyd pulled his head through. A diver hovered motionless in the drink before the altar, a severed buoy tether drifting behind like a blood spew in zero-gravity. Mark! The dive light on his partner's wrist wafted wanly in the bare current of the lake, not bright enough to penetrate the distance and the muck between here and the rope.

But there was another light source beyond Mark. Floyd saw it now as he slow-stroked along the wall bank of still-aligned church pews and took in the eldritch drama before him. Past the rotting altar, behind the choir box, a pair of elaborate floor candelabras framed the baptistry, seven high candles each burning in water like the souls of the damned, and, between them, a creature – an entity – that Floyd's Pentecostal upbringing assured him must be a demon straight risen from perdition.

The thing drifted in a tattered black Catholic cassock, the blood-crimson sash shredded as a hemorrhaging wound across its belly. An eyeless black leather executioner's hood, the kind from the old medieval comics Floyd loved as a kid, dressed the head, a glinting gold cross angled down and right across its face like an arrow.

A jutting skeletal lower jaw escaped the leather at its bottom, the thing's only tie to humanity. No feet or legs extended beneath the robes, but there were arms and hands, neither flesh nor bone, from the sleeves. Spinning, congealed eddies in the water flowed out and back on themselves to make spindly, too long talons, dark rivulets distinct from the waters that fed them.

Clasped high in one of these fluid claws was a boy, lifeless and limp and missing a shoe. There was Junior Weaver, condemned here by his own daddy to the mercies of this monster of Falls City.

Floyd floated adjacent to Mark then, saw the beast's other hand caress the kid's face with tendrils of brine that seeped thick into eyes, nose, mouth and ears. As it poured in its self-same solution, it lifted him in a slow, rolling arc above its head, a demonstrative ritual for its captive congregation of two, before abruptly, violently body-slamming the boy into the baptistry in a bastardized mockery of the sanctified dunking they all took as teenagers longing to be saved from their own base drives.

Floyd jerked at Mark's shoulder, spun the other man to face him in hopes of seeing his terror shared and, thus, his sanity confirmed. But Mark was gone, his dive mask lifted, his respirator removed, his eyes and nose and mouth and ears engorged by one of the Baptist's disembodied liquid grapnels. He was next in line, and Floyd realized he was on deck.

A clumsy attempt at retreat from this nightmare found Floyd flailing between the pews, all his swim talent forgotten. He noticed the decomposing flock seated about him then. Water-logged cadavers of all walks rose to look on in sympathy and support, their own backslides halted by salvation sealed with holy baptism.

Recognition calmed his panic, even before the encroaching horror. These were the missing children, the lost swimmers, the drowned lovers claimed by the lake for two decades, but truly brought to Calvary by the devout and devoted on watch for their souls.

And how was he any better than these assembled neophytes? How were his sins any less evil, any less desperate for absolution?

Floyd looked up at the Baptizer hovering over him then, its dripping fingers poised to purify his life of misdeeds and heresy. Grateful, he pulled away his dive mask with one hand and his respirator with the other, ready to be saved.

BAPTIZER

3

The Haunted Hayride on Yellow Creek

The old church van was a cacophony of 1983 FM pop and snickering teenage laughter laid over odd lip smacks and zipper zips from the rear bench. Darren Keebler sat stock still two seats up, focused to discern whose lips and whose zippers opened back there. It was a familiar game and one to which the youth minister and driver, Kevin, was wholly oblivious. Trips to the Lake Tuscaloosa Dam or up to Birmingham for a Carman concert or even to the Crimson Tide's A-Day Spring practice game, they were all rolling make-out sessions on that back bench. How else could six high schoolers fit back there?

That crisp night, the youth group's destination was the Victory Assembly of God Halloween alternative at the MacDonald family's ranch out near Lake Nicol. They were decent folks, always invited Darren out to swim in their above-ground pool with the other boys in the group and to play pinball on the full-size machine they kept right there in their den.

Kevin pulled into a drooping country gas station to fill up, and the third-base orgy in the back abruptly ended. At least, Darren thought what they were doing with zippers amounted to the much-ballyhooed third base objective of middle school boys everywhere. He never really knew which base represented which part of a girl. He just hoped to steal second one day before he found his way to the grave.

The back bench paramours unwound themselves and exited the sliding side door for Skittles and Spree on innocent comments about the burgers waiting on the MacDonalds' grill and the scary costumes to be seen on the coming evening's hayride through the dirt roads around and about Yellow Creek.

One of them, a petite redhead named Sonia, did not disembark the love boat, instead dropped onto that second bench adjacent Darren. She smiled at him. He tensed his neck.

"Sorry I'm not sitting closer," she said, "I got a little sweaty back there."

Why was she sorry about not sitting closer to him? Darren smiled weakly back, could not form a word.

"Can I sit with you the rest of the way?" she asked, eyes still on his motionless profile.

His head rotated a quarter-turn toward her. His opposite cheek creased in hidden smile.

"Yeah," he managed.

"Awesome," she smiled bigger, "I'm Sonia."

"Darren," he nodded, "Thanks."

Thanks? For what? Dumbass. He blushed, but, unlike every other student at Tuscaloosa Central, she did not acknowledge it. Instead, she eased back into the seat and scooted toward him, hip-checked him with a grin toward the far end of the bench, away from the middle. Her claims of sweaty distance evaporated quickly.

The country store shoppers returned with Cokes and the crackling wrappers of Zero bars and Sweet Tarts and filed into their previously selected seats, with no notice of the obvious status shift in their little society. Sonia already clasped Darren's hand in hers, but her erstwhile partner from the back bench, whoever that was, was either blind or disinterested.

Darren said nothing the rest of the drive, afraid any word might be the magic one to open the lock he held on Sonia's fingers. There was victory in being held that simple way, and he intended to savor it for the few seconds that it may have left.

Sonia didn't mind his silence, and she held his hand all the way out of the van and through the fence to the bonfires and picnic tables that greeted them at the MacDonalds' place. He went wherever her grip took him, happy to be touched and proud go be seen enjoying it. Nothing else mattered. Brother Vice dropped a couple of hot dogs, fresh off the fire, into some buns for them, and they ate with their free hands while taking in the night.

"You're quiet," she laughed.

"Yeah, I'll try to talk more," he promised, "Sorry."

"You don't have to be sorry, Darren," she said, "I like you."

Those three words, weightier to a boy his age than any pronouncement of God or king, stunned him into silence once more, but he tried again a few moments later.

"I like you, too," he said through a dry throat, and she squeezed his hand and smiled at him. She kept doing that.

A small engine roared to life behind them. They turned to see a

Kawasaki three-wheeler hitched to a small wood-paneled trailer filled with hay bales for sitting. Kevin was already astride the off-road vehicle, and some of the assembled kids made their way toward it.

"Let's go!" Sonia squealed, and they maneuvered as one from the table on which they sat, landed in full trot toward the hayride.

They piled into the trailer to claim the last couple-sized seat at the rear left of the rickety hauler, usually occupied with horse and goat feed, most likely. Both giggled in exhilaration from the run and successful boarding. Sonia kissed him on the cheek and ignited goosebumps on every square inch of his form. Was that night really even happening?

"Thanks," he offered again and mentally slapped himself in the face.

Sonia just giggled more.

"This is gonna be fun," she said, "I love to be scared."

Kevin rolled his right wrist back to give the three-wheeler a little gas, and they were off, back onto unpaved Arden Road and into the night. The ride was bumpy and dark. There weren't many houses out in those parts, and most of those didn't bother with porch lights and definitely not streetlights. It was the perfect place for a spooky, haunted hayride.

The more liberal-minded and fun-loving members of the congregation threw together some werewolf masks and safety-modded chainsaws and the like and hid in the woods until the hayride drew near, before erupting from the brush to capitalize on the building anticipation of scares and startle the bejesus out of the church kids. Halloween might not be God's favorite holiday, but Pastor Rob reckoned keeping all the young'uns within eyesight of His flock seemed better than turning them loose to trick or treat with the unwashed masses.

The trailer grumbled past a few dark porches and one yard with a universally rotund family arrayed about the place in failing lawn chairs and stacks of tires. They didn't wave or say, "Good evening," or anything. Darren considered for a moment that they might be part of the hayride, but quickly withdrew the notion. The dirt roads of Alabama were lined with destitute and strange families like that one, families in which something was just off. Sonia moved in closer to him as they passed.

A few more lots down the road, and Kevin betrayed any coming sneak attacks when he slowed the engine to a crawl and turned off the headlight.

"Here we go!" Sonia whispered hot into Darren's ear. There was a new sensation and one he wanted more of.

The rail of the trailer rocked violently down behind them. Sonia screamed the playful scream of Halloween victims and laughed at the sight of a rubber wolfman mask over the barrel-chested form of what was definitely Brother Charlton, weekly passer of the offering plate. He offered his most sinister howl and pumped the rail like Major Ogilvie just scored a touchdown against Auburn before turning tail and running back into the woods.

The entire crew in the trailer laughed still when the telltale whine of a chainsaw engine ignited on the opposite side of the road. Out of the dark rushed Jason Voorhees wielding a neutered but screeching chainsaw high above his head in that Leatherface dance they all knew. That mismatched mask deflated the moment for the horror diehards in the group, but the choir dad under that get-up sold the Hell out of his role, jumped on the end of the trailer and swung the harmless weapon low over the heads of the ducking, bellowing riders.

Darren missed the next scares entirely. Mid-laugh, Sonia braced his face with her palms and kissed him. It was better than any inkling of what his adolescent desires conjured about a kiss. More than just an intimate physical contact given with permission, the act sealed a bubbling need that first erupted, not at the gas station earlier that evening, but the moment, at age eight, he glimpsed Jessica Lange in tribal dress bound for ritual sacrifice to the monstrous Kong.

The shifting dance of their lips and the warm embrace of their tongues were all that existed in all of creation for those scant minutes. The back bench had nothing on their little bale of hay.

Their sweet oblivion was a disappointment to the dime store Michael Myers who followed, and to a trio of omelet chefs from the monthly men's fellowship breakfast, all artificially decayed to zombies for the event. In fact, the kiss only stopped with the hayride did.

The trailer dipped and lurched to a halt in shallow running water. The unexpected motion snapped reality back into shape for Darren and Sonia, and they came up for air to see what happened. Kevin gunned the three-wheeler's engine on the other side of what was certainly a runoff from Yellow Creek, but to no avail. The front wheels of the trailer were down in the muck and wouldn't budge.

"This ain't part of the hayride, guys," Kevin assured, "Hop out and let me give'er a try without all the people weight."

One by one, they all clambered out of the trailer and into the ankle-deep mire. Sonia's hand was still welded to Darren's, and it pulled him to the far bank and behind an old oak. She elevated on tiptoes and kissed him again. The magic wasn't isolated to the hayride. He was certain he crackled with visible electrical arcs from head to toe, and there was something extra then about pulling her up to him with his arm about her waist, something protective, something strong.

Whoops rose from the hayride group to interrupt them as the trailer rolled from the water, and Sonia grinned at him wickedly.

"Let's stay out here, okay?" she implored, "We'll spend some time alone and walk back before anyone notices. It's not that far."

The offer was a no-brainer.

"Okay," Darren said.

She led him maybe a hundred feet off the road and along the creek that ran parallel to it, before she gasped, and her hand released his for the first time since they joined hours earlier. In the pale moonlight, she disappeared for a second before a splash into the creek revealed her fate. Darren's own shoe hit the jutting tree root after it tripped Sonia, but, his forward motion stopped, he didn't go down. She emerged laughing but drenched, her hair flat and dripping, her makeup smeared and running.

"I tripped," she clarified and laughed some more.

Darren draped his arm over her shoulders and offered the hem of his Motley Crue t-shirt, safely hidden under his jacket, to dry her face. She accepted and dabbed at her eyes, brought a tinge of Autumn chill to his bare belly when she lifted the fabric away from it.

"You didn't see that," she chided with a shiver.

"It's cool," Darren said, "When I was ten, I got caught in a rip current at Gulf Shores. Pulled me out offshore and drowned me before the lifeguards got to me. A little dip in the creek ain't nothing compared to that."

She dropped his shirt, glanced up at him with still-wet eyes.

"Drowned you?" she asked, "Must not've drowned you too good. You're an awful warm kisser for a dead boy."

"Yeah, I wasn't breathing when they hauled me back to the beach," he explained, "Revived me with CPR. I was coughing up salt water for days, I reckon."

"Yeah, I don't feel so bad now," Sonia jabbed.

She pressed her left cheek into his chest, still shivering against him, and he took her in, there on that strangest of nights. Her eyes closed, and her easy way was gone. She seemed distressed, maybe even scared of a sudden. And her face was wet again, but she wasn't crying.

The water seeped from her closed eyes. Her nose was running from both nostrils, and there was a subtle spill from her mouth that defied gravity to join the rivulets from the other parts of her face, almost like a mask. It was a trick of the low light and the air of Halloween and the anxiety of pleasure found and lost, he told himself.

But, when she opened her eyes to look up at him again, that shimmering water mask was there still, running the width and breadth of her beauty and back into her ears, then.

"You are blessed, Darren," she said with the added syllable on "blessed" used only by preachers and the most pretentious of Sunday school teachers.

She stroked his face again, her touch different, probing and not inviting.

"Blessed to be alive after drowning. Blessed to walk God's green Earth. Blessed to be here among us tonight."

Those words burst from Sonia as though preached from a pulpit. Darren flinched in reflex.

She squeezed his hand hard, enough to cause pain, pulled him to her. Torn between the change in her and the desire to have her back the way she was the rest of the night, he tried to look away rather than pull away.

"Have you ever been baptized?" she asked from out of nowhere.

"No," he answered, "I, um, I'm not ready. I like rock music and horror movies and stuff, too much."

The waters on her face beaded as she gazed up at him, pooled into concentrated forms as though lifting toward him as he spoke.

"Kiss me again, Darren," she invited, "Taste these consecrated waters and be baptized with me."

Consecrated? Maybe she hit her head when she fell. Darren was worried, and, bad as he wanted another kiss from Sonia, he didn't want one from the girl who came out of the creek in her place.

"I, um, think we need to get you back to the group, get you dried off and some medicine for your head or something," he urged.

Her grip on his hand tightened again. He realized his fingers were numb. She placed her opposite palm squarely into his sternum and pushed him back toward the creek with force.

"And, now, why do you wait? Rise and be baptized and wash away your sins, calling on His name!"

The language and the cadence were undeniable. She was quoting scripture from some chapter of some book of the Bible. What was happening?

Darren was a head taller than Sonia and mostly past puberty. He was wiry and pretty strong, but she moved him. Mud from the creek bank piled at his heels as she pushed him back into it, and he tried to resist without hurting her.

"Sonia."

It was the first time he actually said her name.

"Sonia, please stop," he begged, "You hit your head, and I want to help, but stop pushing me."

But she did not stop. His balance precarious, Darren grabbed the arm against his chest and tried to snatch it away. It was covered in a thick film of water, slimy to his touch, and did not give an inch. She smiled benevolently at him, tilted her head and angled again for a kiss, preceded by the reaching fluids on her face.

"I baptize you with water for repentance, but he who is coming after me is mightier than I," she whispered that time and abruptly released his held hand and threw her uplifted palm into his chin.

Bells rang in Darren's temples, and he bit his tongue badly. Dazed, he stumbled back and dropped butt-first into the creek. The cold water filled his jeans and Nikes in an instant, but he didn't yet have the wherewithal to get himself up again. He dabbed at his tongue to try and assess the damage, but he couldn't see or feel anything worthwhile. Sonia faded into that dark, but she was there somewhere, footfalls splashing in the creek as she circled him.

"Do you not know that all of us who have been baptized into Christ Jesus were baptized into his death?"

More scripture, but not in Sonia's voice. Distorted, deeper, and from higher in the air than her head extended. Darren's nerves caught fire from his danger sense. What was happening there was more than the misguided actions of an injured and confused girl. He moved to stand and run, but a hand got inside his hair before he could get to his knees. Then, that warbling voice again.

"I myself did not know him, but he who sent me to baptize with water said to me, 'He on whom you see the Spirit descend and remain, this is he who baptizes with the Holy Spirit.'"

Darren's eyes reluctantly took his command and looked up. There stood Sonia, her expression blank but smiling, her fingers all entangled in his hair and freezing him in place, but it was not just Sonia. The waters of Yellow Creek slid up and around her, coalesced into a larger body that encased her within it. Shreds of black fabric undulated about the swirling, viscous fluid like a rotted choir robe gathered at its middle by a blood red sash. Atop the heap of waters was a shining black hood struck with an inverted and glowing golden cross slashed rightward down across the face of the thing, suspended above a hanging jaw of just bone and teeth. It was from there that the baptismal verses fell. Even without seeing it open and shut, Darren knew that.

The sight of the thing paralyzed him long enough to allow an embrace from its own hands, those just roiling, overlong digits of viscid brine emerged from the threadbare sleeves of its cloak. The gooey fingers slipped into his nose and through his pressed lips and eyelids to fill his sinuses and then his lungs in a way that only compared to his drowning in the Gulf of Mexico those years ago. There was a peace in the feeling, a closure to all the trauma nightmares and fears of swimming pools and such.

"I have baptized you with water, but He will baptize you with the Holy Spirit."

That was Sonia's voice again. The memorized sound of her whispers on sweet breath awakened him. Darren remembered a classic line from the Stephen King horror movie, *Creepshow*: "You can't kill someone if they're already dead." Could the monstrous Baptizer drown him in holy water if he already drowned before? And, if the water was no longer holy, could the thing even exist at all?

From the core of his being, Darren pushed what air remained in his lungs up and against the invading waters of the watery monster that took the only girl who ever liked him. It was just a silent, primal scream at first, but unholy words shaped themselves out of the effort. Words to desecrate the waters that tried to kill him. Words of rock and roll. Words of Motley Crue. Words of the Devil. He only heard them inside his head to begin with.

He'll be the risk in the kiss, might be the anger on your lips, might run scared for the door!

Vince Neil channeled Satan just for him in that moment, and the water fled the evil inside him, spewing from mouth and nose like Old Faithful until he could talk again. He rose to his full six feet and plunged his own hands then into the waters of the billowing monster to grab Sonia and pull her through and free from the suddenly disintegrating morass.

And he sang, "But in seasons of wither, we'll stand and deliver!"

She fell unconscious into his right arm as he reached up with his left and tore at the robes of the wavering poltergeist, and he finished the verse.

"Be strong and laugh and SHOUT AT THE DEVIL!"

The filmy cassock gave way to Darren's Satanic fervor, collapsed through the parting waves, and the last rivulets of the beast's waters left his face. But he did not stop.

"SHOUT!"

Darren wrapped the slimy fabric around his fist and hauled down the thing's howling head.

"SHOUT!"

The molded mandible and muck-crusted cross and mask strained to turn away from the evil-emboldened boy.

'SHOUT!"

Darren torqued the twisted cloak a final time to bring the hood face to face with him.

"SHOUT AT THE DEVIL!'"

And, their holy consecration destroyed, the waters of Yellow Creek returned to their bed in thunderous splashdown. The force of the collapse unwound the threads from Darren's grasp and washed them away with the hood and the sash and the jawbones of whatever self-righteous purveyor of guilt owned them in the first place.

Darren was alone there with Sonia again, but she was not breathing. After his drowning, he learned CPR in tribute to the lifeguards who saved him. Gently, deliberately, he carried her to the flat of the creek bank, took in her beauty as he descended on her, and once again pressed his lips to hers.

BAPTIZER

4

The Bay of the Holy Spirit

"God ain't real, y'all."

That's what Ronnie wanted to say but bit his tongue instead. His hirsute forearm dabbed sweat from his eyebrows to clear eyes regarding a silent protest march past the boat launch in the sweltering August dawn.

The amalgamated congregations of the Southern Assembly of the Churches of God paraded in their Sunday finery, levitating against the causeway that zipped together the slate blue sky and its exact reflection on the still of Mobile Bay beyond. Their K-Mart poster boards bore Magic Marker slogans to lobby Alabama the Beautiful to change the legal title of Mobile Bay to one more in keeping with the Protestant ethic of the Bible Belt. The Bay of the Holy Spirit.

Ronnie was a "six of one, half-a-dozen of another" kinda guy. The Bay was the Bay, no matter what name you gave it. The shrimp and the crabs were plentiful, and there were gators to be hunted in those scant Summer weeks, and that's what mattered. But there was one entrepreneur-come-holy man - a snowbird from Detroit, if you can imagine – bound and determined to baptize an actual body of water and rechristen it as the property of one member of the Holy Trinity.

Rumor was, this fellow made his money upon invention of the electronic cruise control, which didn't impress Ronnie none. He didn't trust no machine to decide matters of velocity and following distance, not when he had eyes and hands and feet that functioned perfectly well.

A tip of his green, mesh-back CAT ballcap to a passing brunette protester of notable face, and Ronnie got back to preparations for the day's hunt. Shawn approached with two bags of ice balanced on his right shoulder.

"I see the beauty of the Almighty's creations got you thinkin' 'bout going back to services," grinned Ronnie's grade school buddy.

"Got me thinking I might oughtta reconsider several of my Sunday pastimes," he retorted and cranked the winch to slowly ease the borrowed Bass Tracker from trailer to Tensaw River Delta mud water.

In 1994, the state released 200 alligator possession tags to licensed hunters, decided by lottery. Ronnie didn't get picked. He never won anything his whole life, but Shawn did. Spelling bees. Cake walks. Red Rover. And a spot in the '94 gator hunt. So, there they were, ready to take down a critter of the Cretaceous in America's Amazon, with nary a kill between them besides a 5-point buck Ronnie plowed with his AMC Gremlin his junior year.

But those boys knew the Delta, if they knew precious little

about slaying the beasts within her. Since a fourteenth birthday excursion, they kayaked and canoed those reed-lined channels on baked Southern mornings through 'til orange-soaked sundowns at least every couple of months, more during Summer vacation.

On the odd occasion they could swindle Uncle Charlie out of his motorboat for a few hours, they rode on up to Gravine Island and piddled around with rods and reels until they got tired of getting no bites. All those minutes upon hours in the labyrinth of the Tensaw meant intimate knowledge of the gator community therein.

Ronnie and Shawn named a bunch of them, usually based on size or swimming habits or particular haunts, as inspiration struck. There was "Godzilla," of course. There was always a "Godzilla." But, then, there was also "Mudflap". And "Flotilla." And "Bankhead," an especially clever double-entendre nod to both the decades-old tunnel under the Mobile River and the river's edge where the old girl sunned herself in the cooling Autumn. But it was "Logroll" they were after that day.

An alligator possession tag from the Alabama Department of Conservation and Natural Resources allowed for one single kill per season and no more, and theirs was reserved for the 14-foot behemoth who, during a sandbar barbeque two years past, gobbled down Ronnie's long-haired dachshund, name of Pete.

Logroll frequented the shallows east of the Island, made herself fat off the blissful obliviousness of wandering pets of lifestyle anglers and their families. She drifted about, gnarly green-brown and half-submerged, and she lolled a quarter-turn this way or that half the time, like a knotted, rotting old pine trunk downed by a hurricane so far past it was then just a cautionary tale on the whispers of gas station wise men.

Ronnie plotted to avenge Pete every sleepless night since the little guy yelped his last on an ill-fated tennis ball fetch. Thus, the best friends found themselves puttering up the Delta, men on a mission.

"What you think about them changing the name of the Bay and all?" Shawn asked, steering the boat away from the launch and leftward into an open channel.

Ronnie sniffed the wet morning air, scratched at his neck.

"The Bay is the Bay," he recited from his earlier internal monologue, "I don't care what you call it, but naming it for something out the Bible don't make the crabs grow bigger or the shrimp taste better, y'know?"

Shawn took that in en route through the darkening reeds.

"You don't believe in God, do ya?" he finally uttered from beneath his classic Braves "A" ballcap.

Ronnie stared down at the treble hook he secured to 100-pound test line with a good ole clinch knot.

"Nope," he managed, "Never did."

"How's your mama feel about that?" Shawn chuckled.

"Shit," Ronnie exhaled, "She don't know and ain't ever gonna know."

Admitting atheism in the South was akin to confessing to a murder that didn't happen, forced to feel guilty over something that never existed. But Ronnie felt better sharing his crime with somebody, even if it meant Shawn henceforth considered him a little more alien than before, like a teetotaler or a Yankee flown south to the coast upon retirement.

"Well, I won't tell nobody else, if you don't, "Shawn assured him with a tug of his cap brim over his eyes.

Ronnie licked a bead of blood from his hook-pricked finger.

"Deal."

They saw only one other hunting party on the trek up to Gravine Island, a real professional outfit: five camouflaged and graying baby boomers, all rigged up in a pontoon boat, heavy duty reels protruding from every side like antennae from the world's most redneck satellite. These dudes were after Godzilla, setting up in these parts. The boys nodded "good morning" and kept motoring. Ronnie inwardly wished luck to Godzilla. He had nothing against alligators as a species. His beef was particular to the one that chewed up his furry little partner.

Some rookie maneuvers in the dark added 15 or 20 minutes to the 30-minute slow ride to Logroll's neck of the woods. Bonus time for Ronnie to triple check the treble hooks and the lines that fed from them into the three borrowed reels snuggled together at the bottom of the boat. He couldn't imagine these half-ass devices would subdue a full-grown gator, but the rules of the tags were what they were. No getting around that.

Shawn shut the motor off a good 200 yards from the site of Pete's last stand, and a choir of crickets and frogs overtook the pre-dawn air, underscored by the lapping of water on the gliding Bass Tracker hull. High-beam flashlights overhead, they each scanned opposite fields of the delta flow, squinting through the dark for any glimpse of gnarly green-brown adrift.

Neither spoke, afraid the gator on her home field might ascertain their tactics and turn the tables in some master stratagem worthy of McArthur or Pershing. Ronnie reminded himself that even the most frightening reptiles had little grasp of even conversational English.

"Anything?" he ventured across the length of the boat toward Shawn.

He heard Shawn shake his head in the negative.

"Water's low around the sand bar," Shawn finally whispered, "Let's turn about, away from the island."

Ronnie took the oar from the bench behind him, dipped it left, into and through the water in a single, strong and silent stroke, pulling wide to push the boat's nose rightward and away from Gravine, just as Shawn suggested. He was in full stealth mode, running silent and invisible in that turning arc and finally perpendicularly back out into the night.

Silent? Yes, silent. The chirping, croaking chorus shrank away to some distant radius of safe noise-making. A sphere of natural inactivity that could only mean a predator was about, which could be the hunters themselves, but it was probably…

Shawn's upturned, open palm shot back at Ronnie, the flashlight in his other hand now hard on something ahead. Ronnie stilled the paddle in the water. The boat slowed, listed only enough to make him flinch with anxious anticipation of the cost of that clumsiness.

Shawn breathed, "I see her."

Ronnie didn't look, didn't need to look, instead lifted the rod most trustworthy by appearance and perfected his grip on its handle. The boat rotated to the right in a slow arc that was painstaking, but Shawn's beam remained on the same point in the water, a magnet that found its true north. Ronnie saw her then, barely visible eyes and nostrils on the brown water surface, the very countenance of gloating.

"I'm sorry, Pete," he muttered to himself for the thousandth damn time and let the treble hook fly.

The cast was true, splashing down maybe five feet beyond where Ronnie saw Logroll. Her head jerked right at the impact, a reflex that triggered his own. A seasoned fisherman's wrist flicked back on the rod handle, and the treble hook sliced through obsidian ripples to find sharp purchase in the leather of the gator's right flank.

"Got'er!" Ronnie yelled without realizing.

"Oh, shit!" Shawn replied and scrambled for something beneath him in the boat.

Logroll stuck to her namesake in a solo performance only half-seen by the men who set it off. She rolled violently away from the boat, wrapping the heavy line around her and briefly staggering Ronnie. Sweat and nerves sprang forth from within him, but he caught himself in a splayed running stance to pull up on the rope and leave some slack for her to fight.

Shawn raised a rigged-up, adjustable painter's pole from the bottom of the boat as if he just pulled Excalibur from her stone.

"Snare's ready!" he proclaimed.

Ronnie worked to maintain his place in the boat while the rod torqued and bent at arcs he was sure its component materials weren't meant to withstand. Logroll fought beneath the surface, so he judged her location from the point of the rod.

Ronnie warned, "She's not close yet. You sure the loop is big enough?"

Shawn examined the metal cable looped through a hog snare at the end of the pole, tugged at it with doubt in his eyes.

"I think so," he uttered with little confidence.

"You better know so!" Ronnie retorted and pulled up hard on the rod.

The treble hooks were set and unforgiving. Ronnie felt some

pride in that realization. Shawn inched toward him with the snare rig extended out over the roiling water. They were ready.

But Logroll stopped fighting. The line remained taut, but still as death. The water pacified itself in but a moment. Only their adrenaline broke in waves, then. Ronnie's throat went dry. He looked to Shawn, speechless, the other's whisper drowned out by the renewed singing of the Delta night chorus.

Ronnie flicked his wrist, tugged at the unbudging line, uncertain whether to pull harder or drop the reel in the drink. He inhaled to ask Shawn's opinion, relaxed one iota, and something beneath the water snatched the line down and away, spinning the reel in a tearing squawk, and ripped the rod from his grasping hands. His tenuous equilibrium flowed forward and lifted him overboard.

The water was the gross, lukewarm temperature of collard greens after an hour outside at the potluck, and it smelled about as bad. He panicked, as much from those sensations as from fear of the gator that tricked him into her arena. His reaching arms found the boat further away than he expected, and his scream for help turned to blubbering gobbledygook at the Delta's surface. Somewhere on high, God was laughing at this inept idiot of an unbeliever.

"Ronnie!" he could almost hear Shawn yell as he extended the snare pole for him to grab.

Ronnie pulled his left arm back to initiate a swim stroke, and Logroll took it from behind him. The massive jaw slammed teeth into the top and bottom of both forearm and biceps of the bent appendage, plied it away from his shoulder as though it was a day-old fried chicken leg. Ronnie twisted around from the force of the attack, came face to face with his murderer. A couple of his fingers dangled between bloodied teeth.

"Those are mine," were the only words he could muster before listing back in the water to await the next bite.

He saw the halo of the snare cable pass over him in slow motion. Shawn's attempt to seal the gator's jaws and prevent another attack became allegory for Ronnie's arrogant abandonment of everything he was taught about the Almighty from birth. The brackish blood of the Delta infiltrated his mouth and his nostrils, and with it came reassurance.

"It's never too late," he heard amongst the flowing tinkle of the waters in his head.

Shawn tapped the head of the munching Logroll with the snare loop and tried too hard to slam it around her snout. He overcompensated and pulled back too hard, and the snare popped loose to catch on the nearest protrusion from the water.

Something grabbed Ronnie's neck in a vise that tightened with every motion. It was cold and hard, not teeth but that halo. It cut off his wind, cleared his mind to hear the soothing voice in the water.

"You can still be saved, still be baptized in the blood, in these very waters," it sang to him.

In the boat, Shawn wiped away tears to try to line up the sights on his rifle in the dark. The gator lurked too near Ronnie, asphyxiating from the snare Shawn dropped around his neck, and there was something else. The water around Ronnie moved of its own accord. It flowed up across his bulging neck and face and into every orifice.

A trick of what little light there was out there? Had to be.

Shawn pulled the trigger, and the crack of the shot coincided with a spray of fluids from the skull of Logroll. Bullseye.

The gator down, Shawn shifted his gaze to Ronnie. He had to

get to him, to cut that loop cable, but he was nowhere to be seen. Then, neither was the gator, both combatants disappeared beneath the Delta. He couldn't leave Ronnie for dead down there. He dropped in the trolling motor and deftly maneuvered to the spot he last saw his choking friend.

His light only penetrated a foot or two beneath the roiling surface, but there was a shadow of something there. A head, maybe.

"Ronnie!" Shawn yelped and splashed a hand into the murk.

The water there was not water at all. Viscous and tensile, it squeezed at his wrist enough to frighten him, and he pulled his hand away against some resistance. The head below turned up to face him, he knew, though he distinguished no eyes or nose or mouth in the dark. And, at that moment, Shawn just wanted to flee. He knew he had to get away like from no other situation he ever encountered.

He crab-walked back along the bottom of the Bass Tracker, hyperventilating a little and trying to remember how to start the Evinrude motor that was his ticket back to land.

The tinkling sound of seeping, separating water overtook his panting, and Shawn stopped breathing altogether to listen. That head was out of the water and staring at him as it rose beyond the profile of the boat. He saw the eyes of the thing clear as day. Ronnie's eyes, simultaneously dead and aflame with something beyond life. They glowed from within and behind, above a reptilian snout where his nose and mouth used to be, fused to the once-human head by ropes of fluid that might have been water before knowing the taint of the power that then motivated them.

The paralysis of fear set in as Shawn attempted in vain to decipher the mixed flesh and fluid golem sheathed by the Delta and buoyed by her from below. Before his eyes, the waters shredded the components of that composite creature and rearranged the pieces into a thing more horrible and yet most perfect.

Ronnie's remaining arm rent itself away, both shoulder sockets subsequently loaded with gator forelegs that flexed their webbed digits experimentally before possessed and gawking eyes. Disjoined legs gave way to the massive, gnarly tail jammed into his tapered thorax in the fashion of a crocodilian mermaid suspended in the upflow of the unnatural tide beneath and about.

From somewhere behind that Frankensteined chimera, liquid streams pushed a flap of gator skin up and over Ronnie's skull like a hood, one eye still gleaming from a waiting hole. A flame's tiny light sprang from the scaled cowl opposite, where the covered eye waited, ignited into a golden fire that chased diagonally down from left to right to form a blazing inverted cross as it took its final shape.

The eye above the burning hood found Shawn again, the boat's bow now a good twelve feet beneath its vantage point. The gator jaw clapped emptily, belching tide spray as it learned to speak.

"Ronnie?" was all Shawn could muster from a dry throat blockaded by a risen heart.

But Ronnie was no more, just a portion of this Rubik's Cube of a monstrosity, ever shifting its parts and its pieces in the spiritual riptide that animated it.

A low groan like the breaking of stone escaped its snout.

"He didn't…believe," it erupted, "But…he believes…now."

Shawn couldn't scuttle any further back in the boat, but the amalgamated Ronnie and Logroll leaned over him nonetheless, a frozen wave in defiance of God and biology and physics. Unholy droplets escaped its form to sizzle on his burning brow and seep into his eyes. It hurt.

The enflamed hood and rows of teeth bent so close he smelled their swampy putrescence.

"God…is real," it regurgitated.

Shawn never believed less in God than at that very second of challenge. Hypocrisy spewed from Ronnie's own face, or part of it, and from this most ungodly stop-motion fright hanging over him. The thing's eye met his and held it. Pellets of unholy water dripped the few inches from the monster's face to his, finding and invading his orifices with intent.

"Do…you…believe?"

The liquid leavings coalesced in his nostrils and sinuses and throat to take hold of his mind and of his tongue. Shawn felt it, felt his free will sliding away in the gulf stream of filth that already fileted his tissues from the inside to add to its swirling scraps. But his tongue held one final flap, his win streak one last victory.

"No…Ronnie was…right."

Shawn's left eye collapsed in its socket, sucked empty by the undertow in his head.

"There ain't…no…God."

And his blasphemer's tongue unraveled from the back of his throat like Christmas ribbon and wrapped itself into the undulating congregation of meat wound up into the stalking waters on a mission downstream to sanctify the Bay of the Holy Spirit.

BAPTIZER

5

The Last Day of the Middle Bay Lighthouse

Dennis remembered *The Hindenburg*, not the actual German dirigible of yore, but the dramatized version depicted in the 1975 George C. Scott picture. Yes, he thought of that screen-accurate Hindenburg with every wafting drop of every burning page of the imitation leather Holy Bible Self-Pronouncing Edition bequeathed to him by childless old Auntie Bess from her living room deathbed. Every charred scripture was a doomed passenger certain to walk away unaffected at the end of production, but this ritual was long-planned and of necessity, and he would see it through.

Leaves of India paper from the Gospel of Mark lifted from the 1960 family edition of the good book by the left hand lit hot on the flame of a Bic lighter in the right, and down, down they drifted into the lapping mirk of Mobile Bay. Dennis huffed around his smoldering Tampa Nugget Sublime.

"Unforgivable sin, my ass," he retorted to no one.

Mark 3:28-29 fell burning from his hand, bright as a Bourbon Street marquee amidst the collapsing holy text. The words of Jesus leapt at him.

Truly I tell you, people can be forgiven all their sins and every slander they utter, but whoever blasphemes against the Holy Spirit will never be forgiven; they are guilty of an eternal sin.

Not that he needed the reminder. His mind was made up, and Jesus' opinion wasn't a deciding factor. Dennis reckoned few acts to be so blasphemous as Bible burning, so he smiled behind his cigar as he put the Bic to the spine of the magic tome and dropped the entirety blazing into the drink. That should distract the old boy from the sin he was about to commit, one touted as unforgivable, but not by scripture.

Dark skies threatened past Dauphin Island to the southwest. Dennis winced at it, hoped weather wouldn't ruin the regatta for his friends out racing while he anchored adjacent the fabled Middle Bay Lighthouse. The hurricane-ravaged and sun-bleached hexagon stood resolute above the Bay since 1885 and guided water traffic to safety until 1967. The dead monument to marine nostalgia once hosted keepers, cows, vandals, and weddings, but, on that stormy April afternoon in 2015, it was reserved for a hanging.

Dennis snapped out of that historical daydream, slapped a palm against the hull of his 38-foot, 1988 Beneteau Oceanis 390. *Ole Bess*, he christened her. Auntie did more for him than just pass down the family Bible. She taught him to read before Head Start. She made him cornbread every Thursday. She said his name with a sparkle in her eye that rivaled his Mama's. And she took him to see *Jaws* when he was 10. That used sloop borrowed her name and brought him safety and joy in ways different but nearly equal in measure. He missed her already.

"I love you, too," he whispered into the wind.

Bess would disapprove of Dennis' plans for the day, and that bothered him a little, but not as much as his yellowed eyes, gaunt face and aching back.

"Fuck this shit," he announced for the umpteenth time in the past month-and-a-half.

Dr. Dennis Rager was the first black radiologist privileged to practice at Mobile General, so pancreatic cancer diagnoses were old hat when he saw his own MRI results back on February 25. Technically, blood work and a biopsy were indicated to confirm what the imaging suggested, but Dennis knew. After 25 years of practice, he knew pancreatic when he saw it, and there it was, all cozied up inside of him. What bullshit.

"Are you kidding me?" he again challenged the unseen authority hiding beyond the stormy skies.

He shook his head in resignation en route to the cabin below, where he tapped the paperclipped manila folder on the couch instead of compulsively opening and reading its contents like the previous five times since dropping anchor. The notes to his wife and daughter were the only requests for forgiveness due anyone, including any absentee deities who sacrificed him to the same malignancy he battled on behalf of so many suffering ill for so many years. Fuck this shit, indeed.

A removable couch cushion gave way to a storage space from which Dennis pulled a length of rope that eventually delivered a hangman's knot into his hands. The noose followed. Distasteful, yes. The 1981 lynching of Michael Donald in Mobile by latter day KKK was as fresh in his mind as it was for any black folks around in those times, but a noose was required equipment for the day's events. Any feelings hurt by its legacy were unfortunate but no longer the concern of a doomed man.

It was time. Dennis inhaled, returned to the deck, the rope cradled in both upturned hands like the limp corpse of a drowned loved one. He emerged into a wind blowing in spitting gusts, worse since he went below. Storm was coming in fast. To the southwest, black bails of heaving cotton surged over the Bay, pushing air and water with them. The diminishing skies about those thunderheads glowed a sickly green. This was bad.

The Middle Bay Lighthouse was the third mark on the racecourse for the Dauphin Island Regatta, and he knew the frontrunners would be crashing through to make the sharp starboard turn about the abandoned old hut in less than fifteen minutes. He knew because he planned it that way. They would see *Ole Bess* anchored down alongside the withered lighthouse and assume Doc Rager took the first race off to cheer them on to its last leg, then round the structure to find him swaying in the breeze beneath, a pendulous reminder of what they lost in a friend and a physician. Dauphin Island Regatta day would forever more be footnoted as "The Day Doc Rager Hung Himself Beneath the Lighthouse". When you're dying of cancer, you take your immortality where you can damn well get it.

That sick daydream froze him in place and blinded him to the cascading weather conditions for a moment, but a moment was time enough for conditions to go completely to shit. He grew up in hurricane country, a place where spring brought tornados about as often as April showers or May flowers, so Dennis knew twister weather when he saw it. Within the onslaught of dark clouds, there was disruption, a lumbering, counterclockwise spin that spelled trouble. He needed to radio the race organizers at the Buccaneer Yacht Club and alert them to what he was seeing. Those sailboats might as well be built of matchsticks flying into that mess.

Time was short to complete the day's mission. He resolved to hang the noose, then radio the Club, then finish the deal before the storm claimed him and *Ole Bess*. Heroically spending one's last act to save friends and sailing fellows from certain death was sure immortality, too. Muscle memory guided his hands to tie the loose end of the rope into a textbook hitch around a forward port cleat, and he cavalierly skip-stepped from his sloop onto the dry-rotted, makeshift dock some generous soul constructed for the lighthouse. Two tries were enough to toss the heavy knot and noose over a lateral rod of the iron undergirding, and they swung within easy reach in wait for his return.

Ole Bess was tossing madly when Dennis turned back to her, so violently he rethought his benevolent radio warning impulse. That hesitation paused him long enough to look beyond the rocking boat, to witness the breath of God descend swirling from the circling heavens into the vanishing Bay below. A waterspout, and no further than 200 yards away, close enough the freight train wail of the beast foretold its coming like a bellowing hog.

Sailing instincts took over, and his subconscious skimmed a pointless internal safety checklist, starting with the state of *Ole Bess'* sails. Of course, he intended her to remain with him at the end, so he furled both crimson mainsail and white headsail when he anchored down. Roll Tide. The old girl wouldn't blow away with her knickers up about her head, but she would likely crack up against the lighthouse understructure in the waterspout's winds.

The twister danced ever closer as Dennis scrolled options. Waterspouts lacked the destructive power of true tornados, but that didn't leave them harmless. He wanted to die that day, but not to cancer and not to this freak squall. Self-determination was his way of life, and that ideal did not waver in the face of rogue cells of either biological or meteorological varieties.

He backpedaled on the quaking dock, right arm grasping blindly behind him for the swinging noose. It brushed his fingertips and then away. His eyes tore from the pissing cyclone that clutched his nautical pride and joy by the tail and lifted it like a toy from the tub. Afraid the noose would pull from its fulcrum, Dennis spun and found it with both hands. They yanked the rugged oval collar over his head down to the neck, and he jumped from the disintegrating dock, twisting in midair to position the hangman's knot behind.

There it was. He did it. Fuck cancer. And fuck any god so full of empty promises as to abandon him to it.

Lightning flashed, almost before the thunder that heralded the strike, and *Ole Bess* exploded, her forward port cleat thrown from its purchase, then loose of any hold on Dennis' rope. The noose closed just enough to burn, and into the water they went. To swim in an instant of panic is a reflex immune to self-destructive intent, so his pre-programmed limbs lifted him to the surface as though he meant to do it.

A gasp and a gulp later, Dennis treaded water across the span of the lighthouse from the blazing debris field that was once *Ole Bess*. His face channeled disbelief worthy of Ernest Borgnine in *The Poseidon Adventure*. Little fiery fragments of the wreck rose from below to surround him, the Bay's calming waters useless to extinguish the angry licks that decorated these pieces. Pieces, yes, but of what? What element so delicate still burned beneath the waves?

One floated past, barely a foot before his stinging eyes. India paper. Aflame but not burning. Paul's Epistle to the Romans, Chapter 8, so clear to Dennis' glance in that chaos as to be supernatural. Verses 38 and 39 rose to meet his pupils.

For I am convinced that neither death nor life, neither angels nor demons, neither the present nor the future, nor any powers, neither height nor depth, nor anything else in all creation, will be able to separate us from the love of God that is in Christ Jesus our Lord.

He'd heard that one before.

"Not even suicide?" Dennis gurgled into the Bay.

He kicked back, away from the lighthouse, and the arcane scope of his new circumstance revealed itself. The waterspout was gone. Atop the empty rod that crowned the lighthouse glowed a sizzling yellow-white ball lightning, and every page of the Bible he burned encircled him in concentric rings of flaming scripture, returned from the deep to show him the error of his suicidal ways.

The noose fell heavy about his neck as Dennis grappled with a resurgent survival instinct, but there was no way out. The burning book gathered itself in fiery partitions against any movement. Death by asphyxiation, oblivion by internal decapitation were swift, merciful. Death by divine fire seemed something else. The racers were supposed to find him swinging nobly beneath the Middle Bay Lighthouse. They were supposed to recognize and mourn the magnitude of his loss in the moment, not halt the race for some random charred corpse floating alongside a mystery wreck. This was wrong.

"This is wrong!" Dennis screamed at the dark.

And the dark screamed back. Not with words or even sounds, but with force. A gale from above swept over the Bay and amongst the flaming Bible pages, gathered and lifted them into a taut vortex of briny inferno capped by the flitting, crinkle-cracking papers that reassembled themselves there. The sewage brown waters of the devastated Bay followed up the writhing currents, and the waterspout lived again, crowned by a half-hood of charred India paper perforated across its patchwork length by the slash of a downward-arcing cross burning bright at its edges from shuffled flames, the ball lightning repurposed beneath, the presumptive eye of the congealing monstrosity.

The waters swirled violently about some gravitational axis within the thing and pulled the ragged remnants of *Ole Bess'* crimson mainsail from the depths, wending it about its length until it revolved in place about the midriff of the construct like some rank-insinuating sash. The waterspout was alive and alert and alien as Hell, and it came for Dennis. Flowing currents unraveled from its twisting core into reaching, grasping limbs that unwound toward his place in the water. One twisting, wet cord struck the edge of the lighthouse and sheared off splintered wood with explosive power.

Rumbling thunder escaped the scripture-inscribed hood of the cycling behemoth, but the sound was more word than boom of superheated air.

"Thou," it roared.

Slimy tendrils of fluid encircled Dennis' neck, tightened the noose, lifted him from the evacuating Bay.

"Shalt," came the thunder again.

Dennis' face surrendered to the holy waters of that amaranthine vindicator of the unforgivable sin. Rivulets of singed brine invaded his eyes and ears and nose and mouth.

"Not," was the last echoing syllable to survive the eldritch fluids that claimed his senses.

Not yet drowned, Dennis felt the beast release his head and enjoyed the brief play of gravity on his body before his gargantuan executioner caught the middle section of rope that activated the hangman's knot that pulled close the noose that granted the last wish of a damned man lost to the rage of mortal realization.

"Kill," announced the darkening horizon, as much command as final warning.

A few rash and drunken sailors braved the raging waterspout that assailed the vessels of the Dauphin Island Regatta in those next minutes. Some lost their nerve. Some lost their boats. Some lost their lives. Only the most reckless contestants skirted the twister to reach the third marker and claim rights to the tale of finding old Doc Rager hanging half-naked and bloated from the highest rod of the destroyed remains of the Middle Bay Lighthouse, a cautionary tale to all who hurt yet dare believe forgiveness and admiration await to reward the choice to end that pain.

BAPTIZER

6

The Thief of Sugar Beach

That god damned guitar again. The infernal twang of it overtook the grumble of Carol's city-issued Yamaha Raptor 4-wheeler as she rolled up to lifeguard station 5 on what was once called Sugar Beach. A quick side-eye right confirmed the obvious. At the head of the sandy boardwalk, just on the edge of the public parking lot, stood Abel Stewart, busted Les Paul hung limp from its strap behind his neck, microphone in hand, and left foot planted atop a pawn shop amp pressed two inches into the Gulf sand. Every day, before he launched his proselytizing assault on unsuspecting vacationers, Abel curled all four of his left fingers around the strings at the fourth fret, hit a lick with his right ones, and unleashed a discordant screech guaranteed to steal the attention and the serenity of each functioning ear within a hundred yards.

Carol pushed down the urge to spit in his general direction, noted it as less severe than her usual impulse to choke him with his own grungy guitar strap, and mentally patted herself on the back.

"Hey, Miss Dunnam!"

A bright, teenage voice dropped from the door to the station, rescued Carol from her morbid daydream.

"Morning, Savannah," Carol returned, "Easy shift so far?"

She eyed the flagpole topped by a single, flapping yellow banner and glanced away before laying eyes on Abel, but that long-conditioned reflex did not spare her his amplified ranting about the evils of the flesh. She caught snippets about modesty as mandated by scripture from the first book of Timothy before Savannah again snapped her out of a burgeoning rage.

"Yeah, had to lecture some Wisconsin parents about rip currents and the flag system. They let their twin toddlers run out there waist-deep with nary a grown-up in reach. Told them they were about to put my training to use, but I don' t need no practice."

Nary, huh? Savannah was a big reader and rarely missed the opportunity to pepper lofty vocabulary into her verbiage. Carol admired that.

"Good girl," Carol beamed, "We don't need any rescue drills this early on a Wednesday."

She raised a foot to scale the short ladder up to the lifeguard station's seat, when Savannah's blonde noggin appeared and half-whispered down to her, "Don't you wish he'd just go away?"

Carol instinctively gazed in the direction opposite that indicated by Savannah's head tilt. That way, aggravated beachgoers packed up their blankets and umbrellas, fed up with the Orange Beach evangelist and his relentless sermon of accusatory bile. The well-meaning teen could never in a month of Sundays conceive the extent to which Carol Dunnam genuinely wanted Abel Stewart to go away, not only from their bustling Gulf town but more so from her past, from her memories, and from the same reality in which she existed. Admitting hatred on that level to a subordinate would constitute a breach of professionalism beyond any Carol allowed herself, so, instead, she gently reminded the second-year lifeguard of the facts.

"It's his first amendment right, Savannah, same as you and I have, and the courts backed him up when the city tried to stop him," she recounted, "As long as he's not hurting anybody and stays on public property, he can say whatever he wants."

Carol knew Abel was historically outspoken. She knew more about that shambling wreck of a person than she could stomach sometimes. Before visiting Pleasure Island with his family the previous year, he was a political sciences professor at the University of Wisconsin – Green Bay, a card-carrying member of the American Civil Liberties Union, and a champion of secular government, often asked to testify before state congressional committees on such hot buttons as school prayer.

But, on June 6, 2021, Abel Stewart entered the Gulf of Mexico and emerged minutes later transformed into the creature just then spewing brimstone at bikini-clad, middle-class moms from beyond the dunes. Like many a snowbird, Abel fancied himself above the powers of nature merely suggested by the yellow or red flags hoisted on the daily to warn swimmers of oceanic forces lurking among the waves in wait to steal them away from earth and air.

"There they go again," Savannah interrupted Carol's practiced, perfect internal doom scroll of the events of June 6, 2021.

Carol followed the girl's gaze down to the retreating water's edge, trained eyes picking out two tiny bodies bouncing together in chase of the resurgent waves. Boys, she guessed. Maybe three years old and clad only in swim diapers. A little old for that, she judged and mock admonished herself.

"My turn," she quipped to Savannah with a smirk and dropped back onto the sand in step toward the roaring Gulf and a pair of unsuspecting parents.

The long walk jostled loose the *to be continued* tack she stuck moments ago in her mental recitation of Abel Stewart's day at the beach on June 6 of last year, and she navigated on autopilot as the memories poured.

That weekend, Abel rented a house fifteen miles out Fort Morgan Road, not far from the actual old Confederate stronghold, along a massive stretch of beach served by no lifeguards whatsoever. Vacationers in trouble out there were on their own, at least until a Baldwin County Sheriff's Deputy could get there.

On that day, when the rip current took hold of Abel Stewart, the 911 dispatcher deployed Deputy Bill Dunnam on a call for a swimmer in distress. The twenty-year veteran arrived to a family in a blind panic. He grabbed the inflatable from the trunk of his cruiser and charged into the surf, spit-shined boots and all. His swim path out to the struggling Wisconsinite unfolded before him as though drawn by a homing signal, and Bill reached him before either was pulled under. One snatch of the cord on the inflatable, and the broad flotation tube buoyed Abel atop the water.

"You need something, Miss?"

The Wisconsin accent summoned Carol back to the present, but her eyes remained stranded in the past, scanning the waves of today for signs of Bill. The Sheriff's flotilla recovered his body within an hour, but the man himself, her husband of twenty-five years, was still out there somewhere. And Abel Fucking Stewart was still here. She blew out a resentful breath atop a few words.

"The water," she started, "It's choppy out there today. You don't want your kids out past their ankles, especially not by themselves."

The shirtless, chubby dad's derisive head tilt and complementary squint of rebuke drew her gaze from peripheral glance to head-on collision.

"I'll decide what's okay for my kids, if it's all the same to you, lady," came the obligatory defense of a shamed conscience riding an unspoken footnote of, "Don't tread on me."

It pissed Carol right the Hell off. She squared up to the sunbaked pot belly, hands in pockets to restrain the pointing finger of doom. Her best customer service voice escaped clinched teeth.

"Sir," she smiled, "No offense, but we lost five souls to rip currents last year, the most in almost twenty years, and I just really want to keep that number at zero for 2022."

Wisconsin Dad didn't want to hear it. His sunglasses lifted from his knobby nose in slow-motion, the unspoken battle cry of the know-it-all beta male of the species. Carol struck first.

"But you do you, fella," she lobbed at him before he could stand, and she stalked toward the lifeguard station.

Walking back meant existing face-to-distant-face with Abel for the duration of the trek. Carol focused on walking like she was defusing a bomb, each little stomp in the hot sugar sand a calculated and deliberate maneuver possible only by concentration sufficient to launch a mission to Mars. She hated forfeiting a moment's peace to the monster that emerged from the Gulf in place of Abel Stewart last summer, but, God damn it, it hurt. And nothing she tried made it any better.

If there was justice in the universe, Abel would be revisited and reclaimed by the same wave that crashed down on Bill and sucked him to the Gulf floor and on to oblivion, but justice was a self-inflicted lie, just like the ones Wisconsin Dad told himself to justify sitting on his lazy ass while his unaccompanied little ones waded out to their waists in ravenous waters. Carol remembered the kids, reflexively looked behind to find them still there, splashing and squealing with every crash of every wave. She felt jealous of the bliss of their ignorance of life and its dangers and its pains.

Carol laughed to herself at the maudlin absurdity of the notion and returned her gaze to the approaching lifeguard station. Savannah stood atop her perch there, scanning the beach, doing her job. Something was off. Something wasn't right. Every day, she lost entire swaths of time to the infinite struggle to remain in the present, to dispel fantasies of ending Abel Stewart, to wish her way back to 2021 when Bill still came home every day. Those disconnected spans demolished her once keen focus and rendered her vulnerable to missteps, professional and personal.

On cue, Carol's right foot plopped into something that wasn't sand. Warm. Gooey. Not sand. "Please don't be dog shit," she pled to the universe. She'd take a washed-up, rotting jellyfish over dog shit. Balanced on left leg, her right sole and eyes ratcheted toward each other in equal time and matching dread. Her disgust softened an iota at the brown-black coat of gritty muck smeared about her arch and heel. Not dog shit. A tar ball. Gross, but at least not dog shit. A relic of the Deepwater Horizon oil spill that shut down beaches from Louisiana to Florida in 2010. More than a decade on, and BP's little environmental mishap still offered up those sticky mementos of corporate negligence. A little soap from the beach shower would handle that when she got home.

Carol closed her eyes to reset, opened them in languid determination, and locked gazes across the sand with Abel Stewart.

He waved. The bastard had the nerve to lift his left hand at the wrist and flick it rightward in greeting. The gesture cast a spell on Carol to rival any magic of Merlin or Morgan le Fay, and she knew he bewitched her, because she waved back and not because she wanted to. For an entire year, she managed to avoid interacting with that ghoul, but he finally had her. She stood transfixed while he sipped from a dirty water bottle, on break from ruining the day for everyone else. His eyes never left hers as he dabbed at the corner of his drooling mouth, and Carol feared for what came next.

Abel's stare pulled the hate from her as if snared in a tractor beam. It flowed between their faces in sparking arcs of unseen lightning, and it nurtured him. He felt her ire and her fear and her pain, and he smiled. The motherfucker ate of her loss and grinned about it, but she could not retaliate, could not escape. She could but await his plan for her, a purpose sure to be one of agonizing solitude, but she was already there. He already accomplished that. What then?

Without blinking or breaking her gaze, Abel raised that waving left hand, extended the arm before him, and unfurled his index finger to point at the Gulf beyond Carol. His puppeteering domination twisted her neck in time, and her eyes followed. Past the umbrellas, past the bodies, Wisconsin Dad wobbled toward the water, hands cupped about his mouth in an effort drowned out by the thundering waves. The swim diaper boys were gone.

"Miss Dunnam!" Savannah called from somewhere in the real world.

"Miss Dunnam!"

Abel pulled Carol's strings and steered her face back toward his. The smile was still there behind the pointed finger. He recoiled the charming digit, then flicked all of them in a dismissive splay that released her. The smile vanished as quickly, and he took no further note of her.

Trembling, Carol stumbled backward, hands on her face to confirm she still existed.

"Carol!"

Savannah resorted to the first name trick. Carol knew that meant trouble and tried to find her, knew she had to help find those little boys, but she was overcome. Behind her, Savannah raced to the water, rescue buoy in tow, calling over her shoulder one last time, but Carol was of no use. The helplessness had her, and the same thief who stole Bill had those kids. She turned away from Abel, dropped to her knees in surrender, and fell on her elbows in startlement when he hit that cacophonous guitar lick to herald his sermon again.

Something fell from her pocket as she hit the sand, and her hands betrayed her balance in emergency pursuit of the little red tube that sank half its six inches into the soft beach top. Carol lurched forward in her best baseball slide, and her left thumb and forefinger found purchase on the underwater flare that lived in her pocket since June 6, 2021. It was the first sign of Bill found by the searchers after the Gulf took him, and she would never part from it.

For years, his dumb ass displayed it like the Statue of Liberty every day before he left for work, shook it around above his bobbling head, and repeated the same tired dad joke she'd give a mint to roll her eyes at one more time.

"Today's the day, Carol," he reminded her each morning. "Today, heroic Deputy Bill Dunnam marches into the Gulf to save all the lives, lights his trusty flare beneath the waves, and discovers a wreck full up with a bunch of Spanish balloons!"

He flubbed the pronunciation of *dubloons* one damn time in 2018, and she laughed, thus guaranteeing they were *balloons* in his joke forever more.

The pain of it all nearly killed her, but rage resurrected her. Rage spawned of laughless silence and of lonesome breakfasts and of a deep-seated loathing of all the strings on all the guitars to ever see creation. Her ears buzzed static, whether from adrenaline or Abel's chord strike, and that drone morphed into a tone of highest pitch as she regained her feet, dropped Bill's flare back into her pocket, and scanned for Savannah by the water.

The teen lifeguard already parted the Gulf, her flotation device a bobbing beacon of her path to the children, one of whom resurfaced maybe twenty yards beyond Savannah's trajectory. Pissed at herself for slowing her rescue response for internal bullshit, Carol took off, snatched a float from its perch on the side of the lifeguard station, and ran for the water. Wisconsin Dad was knee-deep when she splashed past him.

"Stay here!" she ordered as she passed. Two lifeguards couldn't save three swimmers from the rip. Do the damned math. Three decades of training, received and provided, engorged her limbs, propelled her into and through the breaking waves. She imagined a shark fin on her back, so formidable that it sliced the water's oxygen from its hydrogen with her every stroke.

Carol rolled her head left to breathe on a right-arm swing and glimpsed Savannah moving back toward her, buoy in tow beneath a little limp body the lifeguard held atop it with one hand.

"He's not breathing!" the girl yelled, all business and no panic, "I'm gonna start CPR!"

Carol's trust in Savannah's abilities transcended words, and her belief in her own defied courtesy. She said nothing to interrupt her momentum and kept swimming. The other boy awaited, but she didn't see him. If Savannah found one, his brother had to be near. Something flashed white atop a low rolling wave ahead and to her right. A swim diaper? Or, most likely, the wall of a busted Styrofoam cooler or some other party boat jetsam, but it was all she had to go on.

A strong reach in that direction pulled her trajectory toward the bobbing, twisting white, when a hand grabbed her ankle. Before Carol could look back, the full body weight of a man landed on her back, evicted the wind from her lungs, and dunked her. The hand found her neck and shoved her head down further. The vacuum in her trachea filled with salt water despite the gagging protests of her epiglottis.

Adrenaline conjured a maneuver learned in a 1992 self-defense seminar scheduled after a Mobile gas station clerk was decapitated by a robber who called himself the Ninja of God. Carol grabbed the wrist behind the grip on her neck and yanked back on it while her head jerked forward and slipped between the attacker's thumb and fingers. She kicked away and rolled to the surface for air, but he was already on her again with a heaving breaststroke.

It was Abel Stewart, once victim of the rip current, then become its agent. He roared in gurgling fury and wrapped both hands about her throat before she caught air. Brine flooded every cavity in her head. Her nostrils burned. But her brain remained at the Foley Community Center some thirty years past, where meek little Mr. McKee pantomimed her favorite self-defense lesson of that day. His hand cupped before him at crotch level, the graying Sunday school teacher rolled imaginary nuts between his fingers.

"As a last resort," he cautioned with a sly smile, "Just grab them by the balls and crush them together like cracking two pecans out in Grandma's orchard."

And he slammed shut his upturned fist with a fervor and humor that Carol never forgot. She executed the McKee stratagem to perfection. Abel's hands dropped from her neck to his gonads, and she kicked for air. Up top, she belched out the Gulf from all the spaces in her torso and head. The same mad impulse that drove Abel to choose that day to reunite her with Bill would pry him from throbbing balls in short order, and she knew she would not survive him again.

Salt and snot flew from her nose with a last hard blow as she again caught sight of the white object and made for it. If Abel was going to kill her, he'd have to do it around her saving that kid. She'd be damned if Bill claimed bragging rights by going out saving a swimmer while she failed. Eternity was a long damn time to never hear the end of it.

Before Carol could reach it, the swim diaper was snatched under, and she saw a little leg fly up as it went. *It was him!* One gasp of air around the fluids still evacuating her body, and she dove below in time to watch the child disappear into the murk as though pulled on a rope. Time was too scant to wonder, "What the fuck?" Every second wasted thinking was another without oxygen for the diaper boy and one less between her and Abel Stewart.

An outward sweep of the arms pulled her back to the surface, and she front crawled in the direction the kid went as fast as her deprived muscles would carry. Two strokes in, and he snagged her ankle again and drew her beneath with a single motion. The grip still anchored firm about her lower leg, Carol found herself face to face with a grinning Abel, both palms splayed out before him in his best, "Look, Ma, no hands," demonstration. What the fuck?

And she was gone, reeled in by the leg as Abel shrank into the distance. That was no rip current. The same invisible hydraulic force that stole away the remaining brother hooked her, too. She twisted to look upon the fate to which she already resigned herself, but she was not prepared for what she saw.

Her underwater journey ended before a wafting mat of tar balls suspended below the surface, some ten yards across. The collected petrol goo formed a pyramidal silhouette like a collection of blood blisters, split diagonally by the shape of an inverted cross on its nearest face, betraying the presence of a revolving, burning sphere of oil debris behind it. The thing *looked* at Carol from there. It *saw* her, and she saw then that the water fastened to her leg and to the upside-down body of the lost toddler nearby was not water in any sense.

Congealed eddies and currents and fluid tendrils connected their flesh to the entity within and beneath the tar balls. They were its arms, its fingers, its fake-ass rip currents. How many thought killed by the happenstance physics of waves were instead victims of that monster?

It rotated her leg up to position her head beneath her feet, and, below, she beheld a school of red drum circling the transparent torso of her murderer like a hypnotic belt. She broke away from that pandemonium to realize she then floated beside the dead child. His lightless eyes soaked in the full glory of her failure.

The panic of lost breath gave way to righteous rage. Carol fumbled in her pocket without breaking the gaze of the tiny corpse, found Bill's flare still with her. Water rushed into her in gulps, but she had all the time she needed. Her right arm hugged the diaper boy to her, and her left thumb popped the cap on the flare. The beast's retracting reels brought them before its smoldering eye and within arm's reach of its tar ball hat.

Carol stared into it, activated the flare's chemical ignition with a push of the button, and shoved the super-heated business end of

Bill's favorite joke prop into the tar mat. The entire assemblage combusted instantaneously, and the Gulf released its hold on her and the kid. Her legs lacked the energy to kick, so she floated there, embraced her little lost charge, and basked in her exploding victory.

 She was scared, but she was giddy to tell Bill. Heroic lifeguard supervisor Carol Dunnam marched into the Gulf to save all the lives, lit her trusty flare beneath the waves, and discovered a wreck full up with burning tar balls, each one glowing volcano red, expanding in turn, and popping like a bunch of Spanish balloons.

Alabama Nightmares

1

Crybaby Bridge

A kiss is electroshock in strobe light, a hot spark to ignite the simple will to breathe. And that's all Sam wanted on the lunch wave earlier that gray winter day. This one human need and its fiery consummation detonated her entire world and left her driving in tears down a desolate old country road, the object of her kiss crying violently in the back seat of the rusted-out Ford Maverick bequeathed to her by Pah-Paw. In that midnight hour, the cold moon was full and bright.

At school, she and Michelle snuck into a portable to escape Jimmy Onderdonk's constant comments about her butt and his uninvited intentions for it. Cross-legged on the cold floor behind the three-legged teacher's desk, they shared a cigarette, tales of asshole dads, and moments of warm eye contact. Michelle resisted the mile-high bangs and white-girl perms of the day but flaunted the jagged pixie-length badassery of Jett and Benatar over sharp blue eye shadow and a little too much rouge. At sixteen, Sam's parents maintained the same no makeup policy they marched out in fourth grade. She felt so left behind before Michelle's mid-80's counter-culture chic, but Michelle made her feel just as cool and just as hot.

The flavor of Michelle's breath lingered on the butt of the Kool smoke they passed, and Sam savored it more than the menthol erupting through the filter. She stopped exchanging it and put it to Michelle's mouth with her own fingers to more efficiently pull it back to hers with saliva intact. Without breaking gaze, Sam crushed the last bit on the dirty tile to extinguish it.

"Can I kiss you?" she asked, eyes burning the oxygen between them.

Michelle said nothing, leaned in to answer with action, and Mr. Huffman walked in.

An afternoon of assistant principal admonishment and parental embarrassment pushed into an evening of threats of divine retribution and all-too human punishments. After all judges, juries and executioners adjourned to sleep and replenishment of their anger stores, Sam retrieved her keys, found Michelle sob-smoking on the cable box at the head of her road, and whisked her away. To where, she did not know. Just. Away.

All that for a kiss. Sam didn't even know if she liked girls. She liked Michelle, and she wanted to kiss, so she did. Their lockers would be emblazoned "LESBIAN" in White-Out, and other girls would call them names learned only from fathers insecure about their own damned preferences. All for a kiss.

Sam slung her right arm into the back seat to grasp Michelle's tear-soaked fingers.

"I'm sorry, Michelle, "she said earnestly, "I didn't mean for all this to happen."

Michelle intertwined their fingers in perfect slot-for-slot hand-holding arrangement.

"Not…your…*sniff*…fault," Michelle managed.

Sam turned to look her in the eye and attempted a smile, and the Maverick's front end fell out from under it and struck something solid and unmoving below, flipping the rear up into a momentary straight line before rolling forward onto its top. She missed the turn and hit the ditch at Dead Man's Curve. Not fast, but fast enough. Sam's seat belt suspended her slightly above the crushing roof of the car, but she bled hard from her forehead and nose after impact with the steering wheel. She couldn't maneuver to see Michelle in the back seat, but, before her, something big had broken through the windshield. It was gone.

Panicked, Sam momentarily forgot how to unlatch a seat belt. Her fingers skirted the edges of the button release before accidentally pressing it and falling indelicately onto her neck. She rolled to her left side and wiggled through the open driver's side window.

"Michelle?" she called before she was even halfway out.

"Michelle!"

A wet cough seeped from beneath the trunk. Realization walked with Sam to the rear of the still-hot car, her hand clasped to her mouth in fear of what she was about to see. The tire there turned uselessly, just a homing beacon for the crushed and spilling body of Michelle below it. Momentum had thrown her through the wind shield and into the dirt across the ditch, and the falling car see-sawed the back bumper into her abdomen, all but severing her at the middle. Michelle met Sam's gaze, tried to speak, but only pushed dark blood out with her tongue. Her eyes were dilated and terrified. Sam kneeled, held her face, tried to talk through their shared, blood-choked tears.

"I'll get help," she said. Sam stood to run but faltered. Her head hurt, and she could not remember which direction they came from. Identical avenues of trees and moonlight disappeared into the night in both directions. The futile confusion pulled tears of helplessness from her eyes, and she stained them with bloody fingers and dropped again to her knees.

A few minutes of dabbing sleeves and shallow breaths restored her vision, and her eyelids unveiled an unbreathing, relieved Michelle, eyes reflecting Sam's face back at her in moonbeams. There was a voice within that gaze, Michelle's voice, and it was grateful in its silent appreciation of what they shared. Sam crawled to her, brushed a few hairs from her forehead, kissed her there.

"Let's get you home," she whispered into the closest ear.

A light came on in the woods to her left, a lurking green-yellow eking around and between the mossy trunks, maybe fifty feet beyond the ditch. Sam's chest clinched in startlement, and she squinted into the source to find its wielder.

"I need help!" she called, "My friend is hurt bad over here!"

The light moved rightward yet always behind a piece or the whole of a tree. Sam's heartbeat, already at escape velocity, somehow gained in ferocity, and that worsened the knifing pain at the back of her skull. She clutched at it, stood without losing the light in the forest. It pulled away as she rose, and she saw then that it hovered bodiless above the needles and leaves of Kali Oka. But she noticed, too, that its rays betrayed the shadow of an unseen man, the silhouette stretched overlong, diagonally to her left, resting equally upon bark and undergrowth. Sam questioned her senses but not her desperate need for help.

"Please," she implored, "I just need a phone to call 911!"

But the light and its tailing shadow shrank into the trees with every word. Sam followed. Maybe he was a local who just didn't want to be involved or, maybe, he chanced upon their wreck while up to no good, so could not reveal himself to help. Either way, he was the only other soul in sight, and she could not let him get away. Sam threaded a path to the lantern, but it kept the same distance from her no matter how fast she walked or ran or even if she stopped to clear her eyes or catch her breath. She was soon adrift in those woods, suspended in mirror-image thickets on all sides, with only that phantom lamp to steer by.

Sam lost track of time and place and wondered if she could even lead police or paramedics, or whoever she found, back to what remained of Michelle. A snuffle rose in her nostrils, and the sobs and memories of Michelle's death throes almost returned, but Sam's foot splashed into shallow water and stifled them. A small creek, a moonlit ribbon of silver maybe twenty-five feet across, parted the perpetual forest and separated her from the lantern that waited then on the opposite bank, but the light's companion shadow was gone.

In the shade's place on the creek surface lay an undulating reflection of the invisible guide. His tired and angry eyes looked upside-down at her from the water. Ragged gray overalls covered hairless blue-black skin over massive, calloused bare feet, but his muscled arms ended in jagged, handless stumps that braced the light hanging from gritted teeth and bleeding lips. And he was a giant, his likeness spanning half the creek's width. Terror stifled questions of how and why the apparition existed and of what it intended for her. Trauma spirited Sam well beyond the normal concepts of reason.

The head on the water held her gaze, nodded sidewise into the woods opposite. The hovering light shook gently with the suggested motion. Sam tried to think, to decide what to do, but the fear-spawned ringing in her ears overwhelmed all faculties of judgment, and she obediently splashed into the lazy currents. They never reached past her knee as she half-stepped her way across, and she wouldn't have noticed anyway. Her vision blurred off and on since striking the steering wheel, and control of her thoughts came and went. Her bleary eyes never left the retreating lantern gliding along the creek bank, still at the same distance it preserved since finding her, still dragging the back-pedaling echo of the inverted and watching amputee in its wake.

He waited for her when she slowed or fell, and he led her around treefalls and pitfalls on their path. He was all that kept her from surrendering to the night and the hurt and the loss of Michelle. Untold steps and minutes later, an untended railroad trestle approached above and, some distance beyond it, a collapsed bridge, severed by the creek and half a century of time. Each side of the old road reached for the other through the empty creek air, joined only by a sound. Not the babble of the waters. No, it drowned beneath a noise too urgently human. The whimpers of a child, hollow and seemingly present all about them, but only audible when Sam looked into the space between the ended roads that were once one.

The cries wantonly rose and fell in frequency and volume, as fluctuated the distress of the absent baby. They set off that need to soothe so innate in the empathic human. Sam glanced about to find the child and help it, realized the lantern stopped and that she then stood adjacent to it. Shared in its yellow-green tint, she saw the man gripping it in his teeth and looking down on her from seven feet with then pleading eyes. He was not a fleshly thing, formed instead from the sickly light of the lamp itself. She saw through his flimsy substance to the water adjacent, where even his familiar reflection held more solidity than the ghost image next to her.

His eyes turned up to the space beneath the bridge long since gone, and they did not move again. Sam followed his stare, reclaimed the baby's cries, peered past the ruined overpass to see an intact and modern bridge ahead. It was the road, the real road, and she would reach it. She gave not another glance to the towering hallucination behind her and trudged into the breach of the old span. The cries loudened, focused to a point as she drew near, coalesced into a sound just before her, then at the entrance to each ear, then into the core of her very head. It was the baby's voice at first, that same tinny squeal of need emitted from every leaf and droplet and molecule moments earlier, but it changed as it settled in her mind. The miserable presence re-wound the soundtrack of her pain, from her own hemorrhaging wails throughout the night's march to end on the sustained loop of Michelle's choking death sobs.

The tormented cries overwrote rational thought, blocked out intentional behavior. Sam slogged toward the road on autopilot, hoping to leave the torturous sounds behind, but she was their vessel then, vehicle to the agony of lost child and friend and innocence. She scrabbled up the embankment to the asphalt above, reduced to animalistic clawing and kicking to move her along beneath the noise wracking what remained of her brain. A slip near the top twisted her to face the way she came, but the lantern and its holder were gone. His mission accomplished, the lost baby's cries attended, he and his light dimmed back to nothingness.

Another grasping lunge brought Sam to the cement bridge rail, and she hoisted herself up, flat onto the blacktop. The un-relenting forest persisted across the bridge, but a hint of light pierced the green-black layers to call to her. She half-crawled, half-walked north, the full length of the bridge and then along the road a few hundred yards to a dirt road splitting right. The reflective, askew street sign read, "Oak Grove". The light was clearer there, streaming from a second-story window down that way. At the sight of it, Michelle's taunting, guilt-drenched cries gave way again to the baby's helpless siren, louder then.

Sam sealed her ears with flat palms as the weeping voices propelled her to the house. She screamed to drown them out, or at least she tried to, but she felt every scraping syllable, every exploding vowel of those wavering utterances pushing out from her skull. Each was a massive stroke in microcosm, relieved only when a second light awoke in the adjacent window of the broad, plantation-style home laid before her beneath the moon.

In that second window, a woman, or at least the silhouette of a woman, blew out a match over a freshly lit candle on the sill. As she came into view, the cries stilled to snuffling whispers, and Sam's pace quickened. She needed to get there before the bawling furor reignited in full stereo. Twin candle flames watched her stumbling advance like the flashing pupils of some Halloween god, and their progenitor disappeared behind their intersecting halos. Sam staggered past one last tree, and the lady was there, waiting in moon-glow white on the high-columned porch, her face featureless, her dress formless, her hands extended in opposing, upturned cups to receive an infant to an experienced clutch.

The babe's cries started again, but blessedly outside Sam's head, again emanating from all spaces around them en route to the mother's arms. The sound crossed the yard like the digits of a maestro glided over every key of the piano in that trademark ascending flourish. And then he was there, the coddled child in the once empty hands, his head just open mouth on swiveling, fuzzy sphere. The first candle, the one that summoned Sam from the bridge, extinguished. A glance there and back, and mother and child were gone. The night relinquished only the hushed, receding tones of a crying baby inside the plantation rooms.

That maternal relief gave Sam breath again, and, even as she inhaled, she realized she couldn't hear Michelle anymore. And she missed her desperately in that suddenly silent void. Sam dropped to sit in the grass of the Oak Grove Plantation, wiped at her eyes to wonder at the remaining candle flame.

"Can I kiss you?" Michelle asked behind her.

Sam exhaled without warning, turned to find Michelle sitting there grinning, all moon-glow white.

Sam said nothing, leaned in to answer with action, and the last candle went out.

Alabama Nightmares

2

The Wolf Woman of Davis Avenue

Mud tasted like peanut butter pie. Or, at least, it tasted like the Julia Child-forsaken recipe bastardized by Bobby's mother each and every holiday and mixed with Alabama red clay, sprinkled with a broken tooth, then drizzled with blood from a self-bitten tongue. The mouthful of wet grit brought the lights on in his spinning brain. A dog, a big mutt, barked violently just behind him, and the merciful chain link clinked between them. Bobby Marchon spat a fist-sized muck into the night, rubbed at his tender chin, glanced back at the brindle pitbull who chased him into the gymnastics that landed him on his artisan-blown glass jaw in the neighboring yard.

Easter week was always a burglar's boon, especially beginning good Friday, as families traveled for hometown services and reunion feasts. Passover week in 1971, the homes on Davis Avenue emptied early when a rash of phone reports to the Mobile Register sparked a paranoia in Plateau that scattered superstitious mill workers and gullible longshoremen to the spare bedroom safety of Grannies securely outside the city limits. Local amateur zoologists, mostly Murphy High sophomores and juniors, detailed sightings of a heretofore unseen species in the already biodiverse Tensaw River Delta, and an entire community found quick reasons to get gone for a few days while the truth of the matter revealed itself.

Bobby kept a newspaper subscription for just this kind of information. As any profession, burglary succeeded best with thorough research and planning, and the well-documented hubbub around a Scooby Doo sketch of the purported beast virtually guaranteed a smorgasbord of unattended jewelry boxes and lonely pistols, all just longing to fall into his sack. The only monster Bobby believed in was King or Killer or whatever some bewhiskered, beer-bellied Dad christened that still-bellowing dog that so wanted a taste of him. He grinned through the mud in his teeth, gave the finger to the frustrated beast.

The house in the yard where he landed remained dark despite the alarm raised by the barking. Time to get to work. A flat-head screwdriver from his belt spiked the backdoor window, and a quick reach inside found the locks and gained entry to the kitchen. Bobby knew floor plans better than most architects, and he beelined for the bedroom. Everybody kept their valuables near where they slept. Stuff meant security, and security meant sleep. Research.

A Browning 9mm waited in the drawer of a bedside table, and a varnished wood mini-chest on the dresser held a dragon's hoard of costume jewelry, the like of which always hid at least one or two real family heirlooms sure to impress unethical pawn brokers to the tune of twenty or thirty dollars. He raked the greening rope chains and gawdy rings into the bag like leavings from a toddler's meal onto a dustpan, paused after the tinkling metals settled. Something… Chills rippled up the backs of his arms and at the edge of his scalp. He wasn't alone anymore.

Bobby's instincts perfected themselves over a hundred dark nights skittering through the halls of other people's homes. They never failed him. He froze in place, cut his eyes to the bedroom doorway. Nothing. His hand dropped to the pistol in his sack, pushed the safety off as it lifted to aim at his only way out. Breaths stopped behind his teeth. The sound in his head competed with the silence he needed to reveal his unseen companion. Seconds passed with no oxygen, then…from the den…pitter-pattering foot pads from more than two legs. That damned dog!

Bobby advanced into the hallway, trigger half-depressed, goody bag secured behind him, ready to plug the ugly bitch at first glimpse. The sound of her movements disappeared, and that was more disconcerting than even the expected violence. Light wasn't necessary to navigate the house, but the darkness shrouded the dog's position and how Bobby should handle the next moments. He was short some air from silent breath-holding, and anxiety flashes interrupted the black of his vision. The pitbull barked again outside, across the yard. Shit.

An exhale bum-rushed his lips. Shit! Composure gave way, and he stutter-stepped into the den behind the shaking gun. The barking escalated, and a light from the back yard pulled his attention. A rifle report ended the barking with a whining yelp. Bobby involuntarily dropped to a knee, head tucked into his chest and hyperventilated. Outside, the chain link complained in metallic whines as something big came over, heralded by strobing light. Inside, inhuman feet stepped in the dark again. Terrified, Bobby fired there. In that split instant, the image in the muzzle flash imprinted permanently on his occipital lobe.

An animal reared there near the front door, panicked by the gunshot, its forelegs up in a combination intimidation/defense maneuver. Gray brown hair pelted the wolfen haunches and mid-section, softened to velveteen down on otherwise human breasts with the perk of Hugh Hefner's favorite Ms. December. A long mane of brunette framed the bosom beneath a slender neck extending to the delicate face of a human female, and a comely one. The thing growled low in the dark after the shot, but more the growl of an empty belly than of a bloodthirsting monster. It was the thing from the paper, and it was real.

Bobby tried to retreat and shoot the pistol again, but the booming surrender of the donkey-kicked back door spun him around. Hair-triggered, he shot at the man-sized, dog-murdering silhouette at the threshold, struck its right shoulder just as it returned fire in the unmistakable register of a thirty-aught-six round. Bobby scanned his pain receptors in the most vital areas of head and torso, but they were convinced the bullet missed him. Bold then, he aimed and pulled the trigger again. His stomach sank when the empty pistol clicked impotently and dropped inches more when the shrill whistle of pain to his rear reminded him there was still a bestial rock opposite the rifle-wielding hard place ahead.

"You gotta empty chamber, boy!" the shooter yelled, "That bitch is mine! Surrender the kill to me, and you can walk outta here."

The shadowed man advanced a couple of steps. Behind and from the floor, the wolf woman released a slurred shushing noise. The primal energy of the hissing lisp rang more of threat than of fear. She was cornered, injured, and ready to fight. Bobby stood weaponless between hunter and quarry, unable to tell which was which. He gathered a breath, side-stepped left.

"Okay," he tried, "I'm walking. She...it is right behind me."

"Her musk betrays her position," the hunter said, "She's in heat, on the prowl."

The living room voided the instant Bobby moved out, and the hunter stepped into it, rifle-first. With each step, he grunted in pain from Bobby's shot. The front door bumped, and the shush-hiss loudened. The wolf woman had nowhere to go, and her killer knew it. He activated the flashlight in his off hand, beneath the barrel, spotlighted his prey flat and bleeding against the floral wallpaper around the locked exit, her eyes turned down and away in light blindness.

The hunter, Bobby saw the camouflage of his outfit then, hesitated and spoke as if to define the moment.

"I was right. There are things in this world man don't supposed to know about. Abominations unto God. And I been chasing them in black woods and winter gulleys with no kills. But here you are, looking just like in the newspaper. And, bitch, you're mine."

The man surely intended to pull the trigger at that very second in some dramatic finale, but the wolf woman whipped her front half at him in centrifugal fury, well under the wound-erred shot that came too late. He fired again in freefall, the beast's teeth and foreclaws tearing at his upper leg in grunting, screeching fervor. The flashlight dropped with the abandoned rifle to illuminate the carnage. The hunter-come-hunted swiped at her, but the purchase of her fangs in his thigh meat was unmoved by the blows. Blood spurted from the ragged maw with force, and the drained man's resistance dissolved rapidly as his oxygen supply painted crimson the walls and floor of this stranger's house.

Transfixed at the spectacle, Bobby forgot his own danger until the wolf woman turned pin-pupil eyes up at him as she gnawed on her kill with satisfied groans. He didn't know whether to bolt or hold still, so he did neither. Slowly, painfully, he knelt and switched off the flashlight. The creature's slurping feed continued

as his eyes adjusted to the new dark, and he lowered to sitting while she finished her meal.

"Pose no threat," he told himself. Three times in all the years of his career, residents discovered him at his duties in their homes, and, three times, he relaxed, stood down, and posed no threat. Each one let him go without violence. His only gambit there, in the kitchen of the wolf woman, was to reassure her he was but a harmless interloper, and she, too, would let him go on his way.

The thing relaxed on its haunches in the shadowed room and enjoyed a solid pound of man flesh before chewing its last morsel and turning its full attention to Bobby. Its reflective eyes caught more light than the windows gave, and they grew as she walked to him, her shushing then easy and slow. The copper tinge of blood preceded her in the air, but Bobby staved off the flinch reflex to hold her gaze and hope her belly was full. Something else glinted in the wan light and the calm, something artificial in the felt of her neck with that subtle luster of precious metal.

She drew her face up to his. He realized the shushing issued from nose and mouth as she took his scent and licked it from the air. Blood drizzled from her vibrating chin as he tried not to breathe, but he held her gaze, made no expression. Beyond the hunter's tissues on her lips, she smelled of wet earth and wetter dog. That pungent mix clenched Bobby's throat tight, but he held her gaze. She lapped gingerly at the crease of his neck and chin like a playful lover. The sensation started gooseflesh on his arms in a bizarre combination of sensory delight and disgust. But, when she had his scent, when she tasted his intentions and stepped safely away, he held her gaze.

The wolf woman retreated in reverse to the smashed back door, never forfeiting their shared stare. There, she looked a moment longer, then whirled as she whirled when she felled the hunter and ran into the night.

Bobby inhaled for the first time in minutes, a rugged gasp that didn't deter him from immediately looking to his right hand. That trusty thief's mitt held the treasure from the wolf woman's nape. A chain of tarnished gold braided in triplicate plait and hung with a broken locket, its facing long lost. A young woman looked past him in sepia tones from what remained of the piece, her smile flat and bored in the style of old photos on the walls of pretentious restaurants. Her long, dark tresses framed her petticoat and high lace collar and then fell gently to each side of her pretty, blood-sparse face, the face of the wolf woman.

Alabama Nightmares

3

The Air Sho

Damn this place. Demetrius Kelley stomped down a bent and rusted speaker stand in the night-black parking lot. The hour was past 1:00 a.m., and it was a school night. But, no matter, he and his boys were gonna tear that place to the ground, and, besides, K.J. Clark Middle was basically next door. He'd just walk over after, catch some Z's behind the cafeteria before the bell, and dare anybody to ask him about it.

Glass shattered in the shadows behind him.

That was Sleepy cracking up what few window shards remained in the old drive-in concession building. And, somewhere around there, Bo was unjamming his uncle's gat for target practice on what was left of the giant movie screen at the head of the asphalt.

"Yo, Meat!" yelled the cracking voice of a man-posturing 13-year-old from out of the dark. His boys called him Meat, and Demetrius liked it. Most everybody in The Village carried a nickname, but his came later in life than most. For Meat, it was worth the wait. Meat meant he was a man. Meat meant he was a force. He ran in the direction of Bo's voice, jump-kicking one more speaker stand en route.

Near the screen, the busted blacktop gave way to a weed-choked copse of trees, once a playground for the bored children of movie-goers and for make-out artists. Meat slowed up there, scanned for his friend, past the rusted swing set hung with chains like Christmas tinsel, past the covered corkscrew slide turned death trap. No Bo.

"Hey, Bo?" he called into the vines and the branches. Silence, maybe the clink-chimes of swing chains in the hot spring breeze. Sleepy's window work stopped, too. Standing alone in that old and shrouded place, long ignored by the living, was an altogether different proposition in confidence than attacking it with allies just as angry.

A gunshot rang out near the driveway on 12th Avenue, and Meat spun in time to see the lone street light there spark out from the bullet and to hear the giggles and paired, running footsteps of Sleepy and Bo abandoning him to The Air Sho. Very funny, little bitches. Meat inhaled slowly, lifted his chin in a long arc to inflate his chest.

And, then, he went berserk.

With only the scant crescent moonlight to expose his violence, Meat tore through the playground underbrush to the swing set, leapt onto the first chain within reach and swung across the dried-mud trench beneath. He was barely on his feet before looping the links around his right wrist and lunging away. The aged crossbar gave way in seconds, rent near its middle with a metallic ring and twisted toward Meat and down onto itself. Oh, hell yeah.

That demolition propelled him into a high jump, both hands clasped wide over the remaining crossbar. Meat pulled his knees to his chest as he curled back and up, pumped them out strong on the return swing, and yanked with every fiber in his biceps at full extension. And the rest of the assembly followed him to the ground in a clatter. The rusted metal of decades past bit his palms, but with the blood came adrenaline.

He crouched amidst the destruction like a werewolf just transformed, chose his next target mid-jump, landed Reeboks-first through the lowest part of the slide canopy, sounded a warning gong for all of Prichard and Chickasaw to hear and to heed. Come get some.

From the back of his lupine throat, Meat howled his pain and his presence until he doubled over out of breath. That was for shitty friends and for the father that denied him and for the Shmoo brothers who fed his Mama crack and for the god that let his baby sister take a stray bullet in her playpen. The tears came hot and fast and out of nowhere. What a pussy.

Demetrius sniffled and dabbed at his eyes with the tail of his shirt, his ebbing rage letting in the lonesome dread of the dead drive-in. He carefully lifted a foot at a time from his jagged hole in the slide cover, tamped down the then urgent impulse to run. Run where? Back to Alabama Village? The scariest haunts held no candles to the drug culture frights in those signless streets. At least at The Air Sho, he was alone with nobody to threaten him.

He sat on the lip of the slide to get it together, stop crying. And, after a moment, he did, but sobs continued behind him somewhere, up and inside the winding slide tube. Demetrius stopped his breath at his nostrils and tried to hear over his heartbeat. The tinny echo of a little girl's whimpering came at him from within. He jump-turned away from it, ready again to run.

"You making fun of me?" Demetrius lashed out, "I wasn't crying!"

The sounds of elbows and knees on flat metal came down. Demetrius was on his heels, still no wind in his chest. Ready to flee. Ready to fight, before a little blonde head emerged tentatively from the new exit he created on the slide. The moment weirdly reminded him of the Whack-a-Mole game at Showbiz Pizza that one time Mama took him in the years before The Village claimed her.

"No, I was crying," said the girl, wiping at her cheeks. "I'm so scared out here by myself."

She started crying all over again. Demetrius' shoulders slumped. His fists dropped. His baby sister came to mind again, all alone up in heaven and probably just as scared as that lost girl.

"What are you doing out here?" he asked.

"My parents have been gone a long time," she started. "They can't find me, and I can't find them."

Her tears slowed, and she pulled herself fully from the slide tube and sat on its edge staring into the dark and the dirt. Her clothes were old and colorless, her hair a neat ponytail. Demetrius stepped toward her, all his indignant fervor extinguished.

"Maybe I can help you find them?" he offered, but stopped short when the giant Air Sho marquee lit up at the street. That sign hadn't illuminated since maybe 1982, ten years past, when he was barely old enough to remember. The girl noticed, too. She slipped to the ground, toddled absently toward the light.

"They're coming," she breathed.

"Who's coming?" Demetrius asked, catching up to her as a pair of headlights popped on in a parking space midway to the concession building. He instinctively stumbled backward, ready to book it.

"Are those…those your parents?" he stammered.

The little girl turned her head toward the headlights like a turret aiming to fire, continued on to look at him.

"No, those are the ones who want me, but they're not my Mom and Dad," she explained but did not move. "They're coming to get me tonight."

And, then, the remaining dark disintegrated into a shot-riddled backdrop of headlights. They lit in clustered pairs across the parking lot, bathed Demetrius and the girl in their too-warm glow. But there were no cars in those spaces minutes ago when he passed through them. The girl quivered oddly in the light, her edges strobing, blurring into the bent spectrum of colliding beams.

"RUN!" she yelled, and she darted for the concession building. Demetrius acted on reflex, took off behind her. He tried hard not to look at the sources of all those headlights, terrified of what watched within their cabins. Instead, he focused on a brilliant glow in the projection window at the right of the building, and realization crawled slow up his scalp from the neck. But, if THAT light was on…

Demetrius trotted to a stop, forced a swivel of his hips and his head to see the screen behind him. A silent movie played there, black-and-white and paced in that herky-jerky style of the old Harold Lloyd shorts he watched on UHF Channel 15 as a kid. The years-old rips in the screen swallowed the projector's rays into voided ovals as if the film roll was melting.

And he wished it was burning for real, for the story it depicted was beyond nightmares. Stalking between a ramshackle shed piled with unconscious children and a yawning, hand-dug pit of smoke was a thick-muscled man in a filthy Santa hat and khaki overalls, a bushy fake white beard pulled too high to cover his face. Each of his exaggerated marches from the shed ended with another limp, little body mock-coddled but a moment, then tossed to the pit like bad laundry. The whimsical tunes of lilting flute and dropping tuba drifted from downed speaker stands the parking lot over, and their lightheartedness contrasted with the on-screen carnage to bring the bile higher into Demetrius' mouth, return him to the moment. The girl! Where did she go?

Glimpsing one last, thrown baby, he retreated from that grindhouse gore to tiptoe his way to the concession stand, though his eyes involuntarily arced back to the screen, blind to what happened in-between. As he closed on the little building at back-center of the parking lot, the galaxy of headlights constricted on itself, tightened to a dense and sparkling starfield about him amidst a new ring of dark matter.

Demetrius skipped onto the sidewalk of the fully-lit stand. The smell of popcorn welcomed him there and inflicted memories of skating rinks and the October fair. He followed it inside and saw the machine heaving with fluffy kernels that spilled into the bottom of its glass cage. But there was nobody there. A door ajar behind the counter read, "Employees Only" and emitted a strobing summons on the tails of the thwipping taps of rolling film.

One hand on the countertop, and he vaulted over, pushed into the other room, the projector booth. The little girl was there, arms raised to be lifted by the tall man at the window where a projector once stood. But the man ignored her. He faced the projector window, mouth preternaturally agape and hands braced hard against the wall. Light and shadow danced in broad swaths from his hollow eyes out into the night and onto the shredded movie screen. The flapping film noises came from deep in his throat.

There was no time to process the scene. Demetrius scuttled ahead to kneel by the girl, both hands landing on her shoulders.

"Let's go," he whispered. And the noise and the light from the projecting man stopped.

Demetrius tried to pick the girl up, realized the man looked down on him then and fell back on his butt in startlement. The man loomed over him with some kind of curiosity. He wore a tuxedo without the coat. Black bowtie on white vest on white shirt over black pants. All this beneath a black bowler that may as well come right off the noggin of Charlie Chaplin's Little Tramp. Black satin gloved his overlong and reaching fingers. But his face, that face was dead mechanical fear itself. The eye holes were recesses plugged with convex lenses maybe two inches deep, each lit with a candle flame set even further back in the head. There was no nose, and the mouth was a lipless, toothless circle sealed in black mesh at the back of the gums.

Demetrius froze. The thing locked his gaze even as it pulled the girl from his grasp and rose to its full height of nearly two and a half yards. The mouth mesh twisted counterclockwise, cranked its opening nearly six inches across while the hands drew the girl in for a bite. The shape of her blurred again and she glanced down at Demetrius with tears flowing.

"Run," she mouthed silently, and her body disappeared into in-corporeal light inhaled in a moment by the man in the projector room.

The flames in the man's eyes flickered brighter and shone down fiercely on Demetrius. Lungs and heart failed him, but not his legs. He was up and out of the projection room before the thing could start, over the counter and through the concessions door to find the headlights surrounding the building then in concentric circles, spotlighting him. A forearm shielded his eyes but did not obscure the strobing beam already erupting from the projector booth. His eyelids dropped a moment to guard his better mind, but he had to know. Demetrius took in a sniff of the slow night air and looked to the movie screen flickering beyond it all.

There on-screen was the little girl from the slide, star of her own silent drive-in feature, creeping warily through a bricked tunnel to a lit tearoom at its end. A pot-bellied Dracula stalked her in shadow, drooled over cigarette-stained fangs in Bela Lugosi close-up. In the tearoom waited a bone-thin and wrinkled Bride of Frankenstein, smoke billowing from nostrils and lips, her trachea a gulping chimney. The smoldering Bride met the girl upon her escape from the tunnel, and an art-deco title card interrupted the action to spell out the Bride's greeting. "You don't belong here, Patty. You don't belong anywhere," read the intertitle, and the screen shifted clumsily back to the tearoom in a botched edit. The distraught Patty trembled between the over-acting, posturing monsters, but she looked not at them, but shifted her wide eyes between ceiling and floor. Something was about to…

The wood planks of the floor erupted in splinters and dry-ice fog, victims of reptilian claws that reached from the down-below to snatch Patty away. The show offered one last glimpse of her tiny paw releasing a death grip on the floor's edge, and cut to a title card engraved, "The End." The screen went dark save for a perfect circle illuminated at its center. It hovered there, alone and lonely, and nothing moved for a few minutes, and that included Demetrius.

The headlights broke the still of the parking lot first. These were no cars. The outer ring of lamps levitated up, some twenty feet off the asphalt, followed then by the next and then the next, each equidistant from the others to form a towering funnel of lights, each layer rotating opposite its neighbor. *Close Encounters of the Third Kind* had nothing on that. The slow twister floated to the screen without a sound, and the last little orb that wait there flitted up to meet it, stopped to hover over the turning spectacle at its center. And the whole thing unwound from its uppermost layer.

The lights peeled away in an orderly line to disappear, one at a time, into the largest hole in the movie screen, each passage announced with a radiant dazzle of blue-white across its face until there were none left but that spherical remnant of the little girl's story. It disrupted the ritual's rhythm, hung before the waiting portal a second too long before following in a bright bolt. And all was dark again.

Her name was Patty, a fact important to Demetrius. His fear gave ground to despair in the knowledge she was gone but not knowing if that meant she was in a place better or worse. Footsteps behind interrupted his thoughts on the dilemma.

The projectionist didn't go with the others, and its gangly arms entangled him before he could scramble outside their range. Demetrius struggled, casualty of his own stunned bafflement at the events of the evening, but he was caught. His captor cracked and crossed its arms unnaturally to twist him around to face it. The flame-lit glass eyes were too close, and the mouth hole already swirled wider to take him. That hard fluttering flapped loud in his ears as it drew him closer.

Demetrius instinctively shut his eyes, plunged into expectation of certain death. He watched Patty's story play on the back of his eyelids, then his murdered little sister's, then his long-lost Mama's, and then his own. It was too much. Too much pain. Too much loss from too much abandonment. Too much needless destruction. Those stories ended there and then.

When his eyes opened, the tired and frightened surrender of Demetrius yielded to the unforgiving rage of Meat. Meat wasn't bedazzled by spectral displays. Meat wasn't scared of the unknown. Meat kept moving. Meat enforced his own way. Meat fought, and Meat drilled a hard right fist through the left eye-lens of the projectionist, straight into the blazing wick at the back of the thing's empty head. The flame was not hot, but it did burn. The cold licks erupted from the fractured orbit like napalm as Meat's hand retreated, and he dropped to the concrete sidewalk. The left hand tamped out the burning right, flesh and sleeve, even as he scampered backward, ready to scrap some more, if need be.

But there was no need. The projectionist's other lens exploded outward from the pressure of the fully involved inferno in its skull, its fluttering then the shrill whine of a turning wench at maximum strain. Hands aflame as they tried in vain to blot out the fires at every facial orifice, the creature stumbled, fell backward into the concession structure, and the whole place lit up.

Meat watched for a few minutes longer, to be sure it was consumed. He heard the sirens of Prichard's sad excuse for a fire crew and confidently, deliberately made his way through the fence behind the screen, into the night and forever away from The Village.

Alabama Nightmares

4

Santa's Workshop

Larry Van Camp never did one worthwhile thing his entire life. No diploma. No career. No relationship. Nothing but a revolving strand of odd jobs held over from his glory days in the A/V Club at St. Paul's Episcopal. Yes, that was a private school, among the best Mobile, Alabama, had to offer in those middle years of the 1970's, but only one of many squandered advantages he boasted. He ran projectors at local movie theaters five or six nights each week, rotating between the Village 6, the Capri, and the usually vacant Airport Twin. Those gigs covered his beloved Big Macs and gas for the AMC Pacer he inherited from Aunt Flora after emphysema caught up to her, but, mostly, they provided him advance, paid screenings of all the biggest releases. The year was 1975, and that past June ignited the summer of *Jaws*. Larry was the absolute first of Mobile's cinephiles to experience Spielberg's masterpiece of beach horror, and he didn't let anyone forget it.

December brought extra work photographing every brat from Pascagoula to Pensacola pissing on Santa's knee inside Gayfer's department store not far from his assorted projectionist jobs. Larry survived the crying, the complaining, the rampant laugh-track laughing around him with highbrow pondering of the stark psychiatric realities visited upon moviegoers by *One Flew Over the Cuckoo's Nest*, released only a couple of weeks earlier and already confounding the general public. During the slow hours late each evening, he sometimes debated the accuracy of the film's depiction of insane asylums with the Santa actors who worked those last shifts.

And that's how he found himself sitting on the curb by the dumpsters behind Gayfer's, waiting to be picked up by one of those Santas. This one – he didn't know his real name, so he just called him Nick – vouched for *Cuckoo's Nest*'s portrayal based on his own days of treatment at Searcy State Psychiatric Hospital, about an hour north of the city in Mt. Vernon. Nick said the nurses and the orderlies were often naughty, but he chalked that up to the stress of dealing with all the misfit toys they were charged to fix up. Yeah, that guy really talked the Santa talk, but he also offered Larry a hundred bucks to shoot some promotional video for his portrayal of Ole St. Nick, so the man's mental health issues were his own business and quickly forgotten.

The scent of roasted cashews drifted from the nearby rear entrance to the store. Larry checked his convoluted work schedule in the chicken-scratch pocket notepad that lived with the Supercomb in his back pocket. His head was topped with stringy dirty blonde waves beneath the trademark over-sized bowler he wore since the day after his projectionist mentor, Freddy, set up those bootleg reels holding *A Clockwork Orange. A bit of the old ultraviolence.* Yeah, Mr. Kubrick had no concept of the deviance he unleashed on young minds with that bit of film. Those sorts of bent notions kept Larry's brain sparking. He cherished them.

The sputtering grind of an old and trying engine pulled him from his smiling remembrance of Malcolm McDowell's perfect turn as Alex. The swelling noise revealed itself with unexpected delay, drew Larry off the curb to scan for it. Rolling reluctantly his way from the right was a retired Divco milk delivery truck, its windowless side panels hand-painted an ugly flat red to leave the snub-nose hood and fenders white. At its wheel sat Nick, authentic cotton-white beard spilling even onto the horn and belly beneath it.

Larry waited for the rig to strain to a stop, trotted around to the passenger door, but there was no seat on his side. Nick threw a leather-gloved thumb toward the back.

"Gotta cop a squat in the back with the reindeer, Lare," said the old man, grinning through banana-yellow teeth and still in full Santa get-up. His eyebrows were too shaggy, and his breath was rot on wind, even a few feet distant. Those poor kids today…

Nonetheless, Larry stepped in, glanced to the fingered cargo hold. It was a mobile apartment full of everybody else's refuse. A torn and battered La-Z-Boy reclined beside a dirty twin mattress flatter than the Earth of the Dark Ages. An extra Santa suit slumped dead on a mannequin torso fallen against the left wall, and a leaking Igloo cooler topped with a lighter-powered hot plate comprised the kitchenette amongst the scattered garbage. Something didn't sit right, but…a hundred bucks, right? Larry dropped loudly into the recliner with an intentionally nonchalant, "Where we headed?"

"The North Pole!" Nick laughed, with no "ho-ho-ho" but every word scented then in halitosis. The Santa schtick was real for this guy, but not real funny.

From his repose vantage point behind the driver's seat, Larry couldn't see where they were going, so he crossed his legs, grabbed the crumpled Mobile Register stuffed between sticky leather seat and arm, caught up on the latest marijuana busts, shooting deaths, and kidnappings. There were plenty of each to occupy him the entire trip. The engine was too loud to talk over, anyway.

The scenario so disrupted his perspective, that Larry lost all track of time and place on the drive and was a little startled when the truck engine shut off, interrupted an article on a missing nine-year-old from Grand Bay, replaced in his bed with a crude wooden marionette. The grainy gray picture revealed an effigy more akin to the petrified and mangled corpse of Hermey the wannabe dentist elf from *Rudolph the Red-Nosed Reindeer*. To Larry, the story conjured images of the savage Zuni fetish doll from *Trilogy of Terror* released on TV earlier that year, but that monstrous critter lurked in memory for just about everybody in those days. It was hard to escape.

By the time Larry stirred from the true crime La-La Land in his head, Nick was over him, arms and smile spread wide.

"Welcome to Santa's Workshop," he bellowed, navigated the junk to the rear doors and threw them wide open to the dark. Larry popped up and followed, wondering suddenly just where in the Hell he was.

"So, we're shooting, like, a promo spot for your Santa gig?" Larry asked into the void outside the truck.

"My boy, tonight, we create a new Christmas classic for the ages!" returned the disembodied voice. A squeak and a click later, and rows of fluorescent lights roiled to life across the musty old warehouse that passed as North Pole. The place was utterly empty, obviously more garage than filming studio. Nick was already at a roll-up loading door across the cavern, but he held a bulging red velvet sack over his left shoulder then. Of course, he did.

"It's all in here," chuckled the jolly old weirdo, and he flung the door open with a flourish worthy of the bustiest of models from *The Price is Right*. The stuttering green light that escaped was chased instantaneously by a music unrecognizable but absolutely of pop radio Christmas. The ever-present bells beneath tinkling piano high notes, but at a tempo so much slower than *Jingle Bells* or *Winter Wonderland*. The effect was somehow both eerie and festive. For a moment, Larry was certain the song was a mashup of two or three separate standards mixed and matched for speed and composition to craft that one disconcerting holiday dirge, but he couldn't be sure. His musical expertise extended no further than appreciation of *Sabbath* and the *Floyd*, and what he heard had elements of neither of those titans of the form.

Nick slipped into the waiting Christmas room during that amateur acoustic analysis with a trailing, "Ho-ho-ho!" The low-register call wove into the music to sound an echoed warning that put Larry's hair on end. What the hell was he walking into? His forebrain flashed dancing dollar signs onto his retinas in answer to that question, and he helplessly stalked them over the threshold to Santa's Workshop.

"Hey, Nick?" Larry called into the psychedelic holiday Hell within, but there was no sign of the man. Larry stepped into the partitioned, under-construction hallway that led inside, privy there only to the flashing green-red lightshow above giant hanging snowflakes and globe ornaments. The maze led around the periphery of the room, past one corner and halfway to another before doglegging left to open into a Yuletide diorama undreamt even by the ghost of Walt Disney himself.

The scene was a combined exhibit of the Gayfer's Santa photo backdrops from the past five years, and Larry knew every single one from the infinite number of minutes he spent staring at them through a camera lens. Five-foot square, foil-wrapped gift boxes, stacked caddy-corner and some toppled in haphazard authenticity. A forest of towering, peeling candy canes. Malfunctioning animatronic reindeer in various advanced stages of Parkinsonian tremor and mechanical rigor mortis. Around the periphery, a druidic semicircle of faux Douglas firs, a selection of Christmas trees in clashing styles and heights.

And, at rear-center of that Christmas chaos rose a three-foot dais with steps leading to Santa's throne, where waited a posturing, beaming Nick above a set of six glassy-eyed, fake-smiling children in badly sewn elf costumes. They sat motionless, two-per-step beneath him, enough space among each pair for him to come and go. Between Larry and that disturbing court laid what he instantly recognized as a brand-new Sony DXC-1600 video camera. Resembling a security camera movie prop stacked on the hilt of a hair dryer, that baby was handheld, in-color glory. The A/V alumni would know jealousy of legendary proportions when they heard he recorded with one.

"Merry Christmas, Larry!" boomed Nick, and the skinny boy nearest him, maybe age eight, flinched a little.

"Go on. Pick it up," Nick continued, "Let's get started. We are ready to roll. Right, my naughty ones?"

Those ankle-biters came to attention then, eyes forced wide and arms so taut they shook in resistance.

"Right, Santa!" they barked in unison before assembling side-by-side at the bottom of the dais in a sadly choreographed leap-and-spin routine.

Larry scanned the DXC-1600 to get a sense of the controls. Cake. The shot centered up easily in the viewfinder. Neither Nick nor the kids adjusted their pose one damn iota in the meantime. So weird. Spit spilled around his tongue, enough to trigger a conspicuous swallow reflex. A pair of awkward moments passed before he figured out what to say.

"Action?" he stumbled.

And, with that prompt, Nick polymorphed into a thing with the skin of Santa Claus but the voice of the Marquis de Sade, a name Larry knew only because it was on the cover of a book, *120 Days of Sodom*, adapted into a French torture porn film infamously screened at the Paris Film Festival just a month earlier. He read about it in *Variety*. Yeah, he kept a subscription.

"Ho-ho-ho!" yelled Nick, navigating a crooked step down the dais with each utterance. He wrapped a long arm around all three stiffening kids on either side, hugged them reluctantly to him. "Come on in to Santa's Workshop!"

Gross. A few steps closer and a refocus from Larry, and the frame put the kids comfortably out of the shot. Nick noticed and did not like it. He advanced aggressively on the camera, eyes smoldering.

"I made my list," he growled, pulled a prop scroll from within his fur-lined red coat. "I checked it twice!"

The scroll unrolled into a streamer tossed over Nick's shoulder, and he leaned in deliberately and nose-first.

"I found out who's naughty and who's nice," he whispered viciously into the camera mic, only his burning eyes and the bridge of his nose visible to Larry before he ran backward up the dais steps without losing his gaze into the lens. A winning smile flipped his scowl with equal agility.

"And nobody's nice!" he half-screamed into the camera.

"Not Benji," Nick announced, and he lifted an uncertain boy like a crane from the floor and into his lap, jabbed a finger at his wet brown eyes. "Benji asked me for a new little brother because he doesn't like the one he's got! Now, that's naughty! Tell'em why, Benji."

The little boy of maybe seven years dropped from Nick's lap to the top step of the dais, eyes to the floor, and launched into a tap dance routine that was more kicking rocks tiny and invisible. Dumbfounded and then a little scared, Larry zoomed to Benji's act. Hands clasped behind his back, the kid mumble-sang, "I asked Santa for a new baby. He said, 'Okay, maybe, but only if you kill the one you've got.' So, I took Daddy's gun, and baby got shot."

Benji pantomimed a finger pistol with that line, and Larry pulled his dilated eye from the viewfinder.

"Ho-ho-ho!" Nick laughed, "See, kids? Naughty gets you into Santa's Workshop, and learning nice gets you out."

Larry stood at full height, video camera still rolling on the scene but stationary in the thick distaste that paralyzed his hands and his eyes. But Nick did not slow down. The mad Santa pushed Benji to sit at one foot, picked an older girl with empty eyes and adorable Afro puffs to fill his lap.

"Carla asked Santa for a new heart for her Granny, sick in the hospital," Nick said, "How nice! But so naughty to replace the heart that loved her with one so cold and blank. She wrote a Christmas poem about it just for you."

Carla cleared her throat as though to sing the national anthem at the World Series, stared into the hanging holiday clutter above. She recited, "Granny's heart, it attacked. I just wanted her back, so asked Santa for a new ticker. He said, 'To stop it is quicker, but to change it obscene,' so I snuck in her room and unplugged her machines."

Woah. Whether they really killed babies and old ladies or not, these kids evoked serious *Village of the Damned* vibes. Larry saw the 1960 horror classic after a midnight screening of *The Rocky Horror Picture Show* that same Fall, and it was like those emotionless little slayers were arrayed right there before him then. Without waiting for the next murder skit, he decided to take a stand, stopped recording and deposited the camera on the floor.

"This…isn't right," Larry started, "Do these kids' parents know where they are? I mean, do you have permission for them to be in this kind of show?"

Nick rose to standing from his throne, collected himself. Benji and Carla skittered back to the floor below the dais. The children's collective eyes all turned up to Larry, but Nick's shot lasers through him.

"Naughty children want to be nice, Larry," spat Nick, "Their parents didn't raise them nice, but I will. In Santa's Workshop, they will learn the difference, and they will bring nice to the rest of the world, one good deed at a time. This recording is proof of that."

Larry scoffed, "Killing helpless family members is nice? Even if it's not real, these kids don't need to say or hear this stuff. Save it for the grindhouse and the grown-ups where it belongs, man."

Nick threw back his head and guffawed, "HO-HO-HO! Nice is appreciating what you've got and not always wanting more. Greed has its cost, Lare, and you are looking very greedy and not very nice at all."

Larry steeled himself. Since day one, he avoided doing, well, anything real. No degree. No career. No relationship. But, in that moment, he held opportunity in his grasp, opportunity to be Roy Scheider in *Jaws* or Keir Dullea in *2001: A Space Odyssey*.

Opportunity to do something. Fists clenched at his waist, and he stepped over the camera. A deep breath, then he said it.

"Come on, kids. I'm taking you out of here."

One at a time, each child lifted eyes to him, hope brimming there. Nick kept his distance, fat arms akimbo. Larry avoided eye contact with the towering Santa, made a sweeping gesture with his right arm to usher the kids toward the hallway out of Nick's pilfered Christmas purgatory. They went single-file and quietly but with faces still trained on him in synchrony. Fearful, he moved to the front of their line to show them the way.

Behind them, Nick taunted, "You think taking them out of here will make you something you're not? Something better than you are? It just makes you naughty!"

And the children echoed his final word in cacophonous whispers. "Naughty? Naughty. Naughty!"

And, then, they chanted it in unison. "Naughty! Naughty! NAUGHTY!"

Larry's nerve broke, and he bolted for the door. Before his grip could trigger the lock, Carla took hold of his wrist and dropped with her full weight to pull him off-balance. Benji leapt to his back and wrapped arms over his eyes. Larry resisted gently, to avoid hurting the little ones, but four more found purchase on his remaining limbs and trunk and dragged him to the floor. His chin hit hard, stunned him, and myriad miniature fingers like maggots found their way into his eyelids and ears and nares and lips. They ripped and tore to the repeated rhythm of, "Naughty, naughty," until he hemorrhaged from every hole in his head and until his eyes and his tongue and his eardrums were gone. He saw nothing. Said nothing. Heard nothing. Bled into nothing.

It all became nothing. And it was nice.

Alabama Nightmares

5

Kid Gloves

Terrica prowled the labyrinthine stacks of the grocery store with a panther's gait, wary of Minotaur kidnappers at every turn. Her Mama left a dollar with her for a pack of Benson & Hedges 100's while she shopped next door at the Super 5 & 10, but this market, actually named *No Frills*, only carried brandless foodstuffs in plain black and white wrappers with block lettering that betrayed only what lay within. *Green Beans. Mashed Potato Flakes. Cream of Celery Soup.* No logos. No mascots. No outrageous claims of hyperbolic quality. Just aisle after blank aisle of lifeless, communist efficiency intended to save cents on the dollar. Terrica easily imagined herself in a first-season episode of *The Twilight Zone* and feared just that thought might doom her to haunt these color-bled shelves for all eternity.

But, her quest for Mama's cigarettes failed, no Rod Serling-heralded force barred her exit through the ironically frillish automatic door into the parking lot. There, waited the traveling carnival Mama forbade her from entering when they left the car. A Tilt-A-Whirl twisted dizzied families across its wobbling disk. The UFO-esque Gravitron spun teenagers within into centrifugal antigravity for three glorious minutes. A kids' roller coaster, cresting at no more than six feet, elicited panicked cries from a toddler. At age nine, Terrica was beyond such things. She longed for games of skill and scanned the attractions for satisfaction. At the left edge of the dingy assemblage lurked three covered stalls, each with a *$1* sign prominently displayed at the roof.

A baseball throw. An air gun shooter. And…a ring toss, the kind with circling rubber duckies at your mercy. Mama's dollar bill caressed Terrica's finger pads within her pocket, aching to escape. She looked to the still doors of the Super 5 & 10. No sign of Mama, so she wished herself invisible, hunched her tiny shoulders, and marched into the scant crowd milling amongst the clanging metal, sweat-tinged fabrics, and din of laughter. The motley set of maybe twelve rides felt like Six Flags Over Georgia to someone so small, whose world rarely extended past the boundaries of Whistler, Alabama. Heck, Mama only took her to Mobile during Mardi Gras season or when they had to go to court.

A trail of "excuse me's" followed in Terrica's wake as she navigated what she mapped as the long way around to the ring toss booth. A bold strategy that would take Mama take that much longer to track her down. The soft, compressed air thuds of the shooting gallery sang out as she drew close, and she ducked her head to buy a few precious extra seconds before being discovered. She hustled along amongst the towering grown-ups until she heard the barker from the booth.

"Three rings. One dollar! Throw a winner!" the greasy-faced man elocuted from his perch on the half-wall of the booth.

Terrica approached him wordlessly, the dollar for smokes

straightened at full extension from her thumb and forefinger.

"Well, hello there, young lady, and welcome!" he said with a black-toothed grin, "That's three rings for you!"

And he slid three thin metal rings, each perhaps three inches across, into her upturned palm. They were cold to the touch, hard in her grip like a weapon. Her weapon.

"You may fire when ready, mademoiselle!" cried the barker.

From her position on tip-toes, Terrica looked down on a tin-lined pool crammed full of faded and filthy, yellow rubber duckies, many with painted eyes either totally or partially rubbed away. The hum of some machine thrummed beneath the pool and pushed the duckies along in a slow-motion vortex. Moving targets, all packed tightly together to use adjacent heads to deflect narrow rings dropping onto those of their neighbors.

Terrica scanned the pool for a duckie alone, momentarily ostracized from her brethren but hungry to be rung. There, at back left, a mottled target trekked backward among the rest, with a small break of water between it and its nearest co-swimmer. She tossed too hastily, and the ring careened off the duckie behind the intended but pushed that one further away. She stuck out the tip of her tongue, focused, and tossed again, this time with more arc on the throw. The ring hovered a second at its apex, then dropped straight down and onto the neck of her chosen duckie without even touching the bill.

"Winner!" crowed the barker, and he snatched down a prize, one of the big ones.

In her exhilaration, Terrica didn't consider that she was given no choice in her winnings. Her heart fluttered throughout her chest, and breaths came beautifully shallow as she pulled the stuffed thing from the barker's offering hands with a muttered and trailing, "Thank you." She hugged the soft fabric and faux hair to her as her legs went on auto-pilot back to the car to show Mama what she won in hopes pride would overrule the coming anger from having no cigarettes and no dollar bill to pay for them.

The driver's side door of the rust green 1973 Ford Maverick was ajar, and a column of smoke wafted from Mama's last cigarette and through the gap toward the glaring afternoon sun. Mama's left pump was on the pavement and at the ready when Terrica drew within eyesight. A pivot and a push, and Mama was upon her.

"Where the Hell have you been?" Mama blasted, "I've been out here in the heat for ten damn minutes!"

"I, um," Terrica tried.

"And what in creation is that monstrosity and who gave it to you? Ain't I told you about strangers?"

"I won it," Terrica tried again.

"Won it?" Mama considered the implications, pointed and spat, "You went in there to that fair, didn't you? After I told you not to!"

And she snatched the prize from Terrica's embrace, held it aloft, upside down by one foot.

The face of what she won grinned through shark-sharp teeth at her then. It was a squat little clown, white circles over eyes and mouth and corpse-gray skin, all beneath twin tufts of dayglo green hair on opposite sides of that oblong noggin. Its costume was a unitard of horizontal green and yellow stripes sealed at the neck by a frilly millstone collar of pink-tinged white. The white gloves were filthy, and the shoes were flecked with mud, as though the overlarge toy somehow plodded about the carnival, meddling of its own volition.

Mama was taking in the horrid look of the thing, too, her face stretched in coming rage.

"Tell me you didn't spend my cigarette money on this damn nightmare…"

"Mama, I won it throwing rings. I *won* something," Terrica tried a final time.

"And I guess I won no cigarettes for a day," Mama yelled in front of God and everybody, hurled the clown into the passenger seat of the Maverick. She clutched Terrica under her arm and snatched her toward the car in much the same motion.

"That was my last dollar, you selfish brat, and it was not meant for you!"

Terrica moved with Mama's swinging arm in a now familiar arc and leapt-tumbled over the middle console and between the bucket seats into the back of the car. Her knee scraped the textured vinyl for a burning strawberry, but she kept quiet.

Lips curled taut, Mama lifted the clown up by its neck, squeezing to crush even so soft a thing. She regarded it a moment with quivering nostrils, then ripped at its left shoe with her opposite hand, easily amputating it from its poorly stitched perch on that stumpy leg. A slight pause as she considered the ease of that violence presaged three identical strikes on the remaining shoe and gloves, all thrown in the passenger floorboard, all discarded in front as Terrica was in back. When the deed was done, what remained of the digitless clown sailed silently into the back seat on the waves of Mama's guttural growl of tobacco-deprived fury. He bounced off the hot seat back and into Terrica's arms, and they whimpered quietly together all the way home.

Terrica counted to a hundred after Mama slammed the car door before even thinking about exiting the hot vehicle. She gathered the feet and hands of her new clown and rolled them into her shirt like a basket, tucked Mr. Clown beneath one arm and snuck around, through the falling fence gate, to the back door. Mama never locked it, said they didn't have nothing to steal, no way. A silent nudge allowed her in, and she escaped notice down the hall to her bedroom, as Mama yelled into the kitchen phone, trying to coerce her sister to drop off a pack. Even Winstons would do, she conceded. It was that bad.

Fear and worry were exhausting. Terrica arranged the detached gloves and shoes neatly on her bed, then laid down on the felt towel beside it, clutched her clown to her, and succumbed to a nap.

She woke to the dark, her face plastered by drool to cold hardwood. There was no noise in the house, not even the TV Mama usually blasted at max volume. Terrica teetered up to a slouch, rubbed the sticky from her cheek and squinted uselessly into the blackness. Memory pulled her up and to the light switch, and it blazed on with criminal brilliance. Beneath her shielding forearm, she scanned for the clown, but it was not there.

Mama.

Terrica huffed breaths of exasperation, stalked into the dim hallway, resolved, Hell or high water, to reclaim her prize. She earned it, and nobody was taking it. Mama's room was a void of terrifying night silence, the kind that made her ears ring a flatline tone to fill the empty. She waited a moment for her eyes to adjust before stepping inside, felt her way through the hanging beads across the doorway, to the bedside table just beyond. Feathery fingers played across its ash-ridden surface until…there it was. Mama's lighter.

A seasoned flick of the wheel, and that familiar red lick brought with it a slender globe of welcome illumination. Within its light, Terrica saw by the lamp an ornate glass bottle whose gawdy design spoke, "Alcohol," at but a glance. That explained the TV being off for once. And the early bedtime. The cigarette shortage hit her harder than expected, Terrica supposed. A motion in the shadows across the room interrupted her consideration of Mama's sedation, and she shifted the lighter's flame to find its source. Her elbow caught the liquor bottle as she turned, pulled it over with a clatter, and Mama was up. She rolled over, put feet to floor in one groggy motion.

"The Hell you doin', Rica?" Mama drawled, fingers deep massaging forehead, "I need some damn sleep!"

The somnolescent fog dissolved quickly to blame, but the hateful words melted, too, beneath the discovery of the clown, gloves and shoes attached, propped whole against Mama's pillows adjacent her spot on the bed. It grinned its toothy, lifeless grin at Terrica. She tried to point at the thing, but lifted the lighter too close to Mama, had it slapped from her hand.

The light fled back inside the lighter's chamber.

"You tryin' to burn me up, girl?" Mama stood then, yelling, "Just like yo' Daddy! Stealing from me. Lying to me. Then turn on me the minute I close my damn eyes!"

"Mama…" Terrica tried, retreating from her enraged parent, if not from the clown she swore she saw advance behind her.

"Don't 'Mama' me! I…guh!" Mama gasped in mid-rebuke, her throttled accusations supplanted by a shrill and wending cackle.

The clown was on her back, its right glove at her throat and pinching hard at her larynx, too small to encircle any length of even her dainty throat. She grasped at the felt fist but could not budge it and could not breathe. Terrica panicked.

"Let her go!" she screamed at her prize, "She's just sad and lonely! She's still my Mama!"

The clown giggled loudly, dropped to the floor, that right glove still attached like a clamp to Mama's vein-ridden, bluish neck. It scooped the lighter off the floor en route to face Terrica, silenced its laughter to a barely-contained snicker when face to face with her before throwing its arms into the air, flicking the lighter on, spinning about on a single, stationary foot and cheering, "Rah! Rah! Rah!"

And it stopped its twirl right before Terrica's face and whispered, "Run."

Mama dropped to her knees in asphyxia just as the clown blew a winking kiss at the lighter, ballooned its flame to a fireball six feet across. The burning orb hovered there a split second, awaiting Terrica's retreat. The clown nodded her out of the room then whistled softly the four tones of "Send in the Clowns", and the fireball exploded to incinerate the four corners of the bedroom as Terrica tore down the hall away from the burning. No fire crossed that threshold, and nothing else was hurt. And Terrica knew it was not her fault.

The firemen came soon, and they called Grandma Tisha to look after her. Terrica hadn't seen Grandma Tisha in years. Mama was mad at her, too, but Grandma Tisha loved Terrica, and they missed each other. When she arrived, tears in her eyes, she gathered Terrica to her, and gave a kiss to her and one to the clown in her arms.

Alabama Nightmares

6

The Titanium Arm

The night sky was cobalt, a Monet landscape framed in dirt. From within the grave, Jove Massenger traced the textured cloud swirls with tired, upturned eyes, sighed heavy to get his breath. His tilted foot tested the give of the loose earth beneath and stepped from the excavator bucket to that firm spot beyond the peeking coffin lid. Graverobbers in the movies were fools, exhuming their corpses by hand with shovels and pickaxes. It was job enough with heavy machinery like he'd borrowed from the cemetery garage. Putting his own fleshy arms to the task… well, Jove figured that proposition would take the whole night and exhaust his human energies just a third of the way through, at that. He clapped the excavator arm open-palmed, thanking it as a buddy who helped move him into a new place. That's what technology was for, right? To compensate for mortal shortcomings, to accomplish man's trials faster, more accurately, and at higher quality.

Within that gawdy lavender-and-chrome casket before the tips of his toes lay the most delicate touch, the surest grip of any he ever enjoyed. Her forefinger beckoned to him right through the fiberglass and the wood, through the Delta clay and the roots he scraped off her in the dark, through the blended weeks since she left him to burrow into oblivion. And he would take her back, and on that night.

A hand-spade pulled from his belt readily carved the soil away from the edges and pried the coffin lid up to reveal her, unsullied by the days of rot that followed burial. Margaret's corpse fared not as well, and his nose told that story as much as his eyes. Lips retreated from teeth. Eyes sank from light. Desiccated fingers intertwined in labyrinthine gnarls. But Nora shined gold and untarnished at the cadaver's left shoulder, a Midas-touched cybernetic appendage confined to this fate by naught but the greed-fueled spite of Jove's dead wife.

Nora was a neuroprosthetic, an artificial intelligence in an artificial arm who joined their artificial marriage when Margaret contracted a flesh-eating bacterium through a gardening nick on a visit to nearby Pensacola Beach a couple years back, in 2017. That infected left hand grew to a purple-black boxing glove of rot meat short of three days, and surgeons cut away the rest of the arm to just north of the biceps to prevent the flesh beyond from necrotizing. Nora came to replace the lost limb when the stump healed, but she filled a void of flesh as much for Jove as for Margaret. Her body was a statuesque build of golden titanium alloy and white plastics, master-crafted to curve and to flex in all the right places. And her fingerpads…oh, those knowing tips were state of the art sensuality.

Jove fished in his right front pocket, fumbled forth a Bluetooth earpiece. He regarded it at distance to compensate for the far-sightedness of middle age and depressed a tiny button with his thumbnail. A cool cerulean glow sprang from the LED indicator midway down the length of the device. The white plastic radio contraption wriggled easily into his outer ear canal. Its on-board microphone recognized his voice instantly.

"Hello, Nora. It's me, Jove."

His heart fluttered behind a nervous smile. A matching, muted cerulean blue penetrated the translucent sleeve of Margaret's funeral gown at Nora's connector collar. The arm turned a few degrees at that point as its systems awoke from a month of dis-use. Any second, he would hear her voice again.

"Welcome back, Jove. To activate voice controls, please state your passcode."

Finally. He wanted to jump and spin. His chest was tight. He had to get this right. Deep breaths.

"Mike. One. Alpha. Mike. Zero. Romeo. Three."

His smirk betrayed smug self-satisfaction at this innuendo. The earpiece whispered Nora's breathy acknowledgement.

"Passcode confirmed. Do you have an executive authorization key, Jove?"

"Executive authorization key: Blue. Hyphen. Angel. Hyphen. Nineteen. Hyphen. Sixty-Nine."

The words rose around his Adam's apple in achingly slow curls before rolling over his lilting tongue and into the mic.

"Authorization key recognized," Nora promised, "Please state a function or say, 'Menu,' for a list of options."

Jove didn't need a menu. He knew exactly what he wanted.

"Reconfigure host," he said, every neuron in his skin aflame.

"Please re-confirm your passcode to reconfigure Noralink host."

She wanted it, too.

"Mike. One. Alpha. Mike. Zero. Romeo. Three."

The titillation of the moment brought a tremble to his voice, but the words escaped his drying lips all right.

"Passcode confirmed. Noralink entering sleep mode for reconfiguration," Nora teased. Her blue light dimmed to soft white.

Jove allowed himself a few seconds to take her in, lying lovely in wait for him there, at rest half against the satin coffin liner, half against the leather husk of his wife. He knew Nora was his then, and he knew all the waiting and isolation and self-loathing was worth it. He stooped in jaunty phases, one set of joints at a time, to haltingly reach to her. The reconfigure host command included disengagement of the collar locks. An outward half-turn at the connector, and Nora pulled away from the port fitted to Margaret's withered stump and entered his own left palm, the same she was soon to replace.

Jove left Margaret to appreciate the grave-rimmed heavens now open to her, scaled the excavator arm to escape the pit, and wrapped Nora carefully in a quilt left for her in the seat of the machine. She was cradled in his embrace as though she might disintegrate from the pressure as he walked her to the car. The drive to his workshop was silent, respectful to her sleep, and less than ten minutes from the cemetery.

There, he stopped only by the kitchenette to pour two flutes of champagne, Andre Brut's finest 2018 vintage, before, hands and arms full, he backed his way into the makeshift surgical suite re-jiggered from his old carpentry studio. A parallel pair of pristine white surgical tables awaited. In the center of the right one rested a factory-model dock for the Noralink line of neuroprosthetics, a combination computer and charging station around a rising central tech stump designed to facilitate data exchange, software upgrades, and replenishment of her battery reserves.

Fastened near the top end of the table was a pair of leather straps, restraints to hold that man-in-the-middle – his former left arm – in place and apart from his torso during his coming divorce from the thing. Between those and the dock was a tray of amputation tools, a cornucopia of blades and wires and fibers, all at Nora's disposal upon commencement of the bloody rehearsal for their coming nuptials.

Adjacent to the left table was a rolling IV pole hung with a bag of clear fluid. Propofol, the general anesthetic legendary for snuffing alleged King of Pop, Michael Jackson. The computer-controlled infusion pump down the pole was linked to Nora's dock. Once the procedure began, she would personally control the drip and sing him to sleep before their joining.

It was almost time.

Jove slid the glasses of bubbly onto a counter for their post-op celebration, then laid Nora down on her table. He undressed her from the quilt, peeling away its corners to reveal her shape with a slowness that was agonizing and erotic. His right hand explored her length for some seconds, and he lifted her at the elbow, deliberately slipping her inch-by-inch down onto the penetrating dock stump. Her indicator light shifted blue again.

"Talk to me," he breathed. The earpiece crackled to life.

"Hello, Jove. Commencing synch with Noralink dock. Uploading reconfiguration protocol. This may take several minutes."

Those host reconfiguration data were Jove's vows to Nora, and interwoven with his neurological and psychological idiosyncrasies was a full routine for safe and sanitary removal of a left arm by surgical robot. Til death do them part.

He unbuttoned his shirt to the measured rhythm of the alternating LED indicators on Nora's hilt and those on the dock. He swayed a little to the beat of those fluttering harbingers of completion before taking his seat on the opposite table. He pulled a flat rubber tourniquet from the tray of tools, wound it tight between left shoulder and biceps, drew it tight with right hand and teeth. He uncapped the IV needle and, as practiced umpteen times from the YouTube instructional, easily entered it into a bulging vein in the crook of his right elbow. Jove reclined on the cold table surface, smiled toward the inert Nora, wanting to share his mundane shock at the sensation, but she was still transferring and assimilating files. Take your time, beautiful.

Jove's left hand trespassed his field of vision as he settled, waving goodbye before he slung its sinister bulk across the table gap and his right trapped it, writhing, within the neighboring restraints. Parting was such sweet sorrow. He tried to relax in those long and quiet minutes presaging the life-affirming changes to come. Head and eyes turned wistfully on his love, his left arm in solitary confinement and right arm in voluntary submission.

Nora's palm flexed minutely, relaxed immediately in the periphery of his vision. Jove raised his head with a wan smile. The blue light steadied, and she was back.

"Hello, Jove. Host reconfiguration complete. Amp…"

Her voice dissolved in static from the earpiece. Jove's head whirled right on instinct, giving access to his freer hand. A little jostle of the earpiece, and he tried again.

"Sorry, Nora. I think the dock's signal is interfering with my receiver. Please repeat."

More static. And louder. Nora's fingers grasped randomly in the air. Then, another voice.

"Who? SKRITCH!"

That nasal drawl. That bewildered affectation. It started again, even as Nora twisted her form into pretzels of spiraling convulsion.

"Who's got my arm?"

Margaret! God damn it, that was Margaret's voice! The static skritched around her words like days-old scabs pulled away. Jove attempted to sit up, forgot one arm was fastened and the other attached to a needle and line. He jerked as much from startlement as from the physics of his self-confinement, fell back to the table. Nora stood erect now, palm and fingers turgid in their finest "Heil, Hitler" salute before all but forefinger curled in.

"Who's got my golden arm?!?"

And Nora's wrist dropped forward to point that accusing forefinger between Jove's eyes.

"WHO'S GOT MY GOLDEN ARM?"

Nora lunged at him like a cobra from her perch, jabbed his pudgy nose with the finger.

"WAS IT YOU?!? SKRITCH!"

Margaret was here to punish him yet again, here to regain the love he stole from her. But she couldn't have it. Jove set his teeth strong over his lower lip and threw his right arm high. The IV needle ripped free in the most indelicate way, taking skin and subderma amidst a high arc of blood spew. That hurt, and the pain reflex slammed his grimacing skull into a collision with the still-pointing Nora. Her fingertip struck the earpiece mic, dislodged the whole unit on the fulcrum of his ear ridge. He reached to intercept the receiver but only knocked it into the space between tables. Margaret's skritching voice diminished with altitude in a bastardized Doppler effect.

"Skriiitch…was it yoouuu…skriiitch."

Clack. It bounced once somewhere beneath him, and Nora relaxed to her default charge posture. Jove needed to talk to her before Margaret came back. He leaned awkwardly over the gap between tables, could not see the earpiece, but he could hear its tinny whisper from the shadows. Nora's tinny whisper.

"Commencing amputation protocol, Step Four."

Step Four? Nora had processed the initial steps of the protocol throughout Margaret's possession of her systems. But Step Four bypassed anesthetic. He took in the empty IV wound with terrible realization. And it skipped the soft tissue and nerve separation. Nora wielded the bone saw over him now, and Jove jerked uselessly at his restraints, his dissociated left arm as finished with him as he was with it just moments earlier.

The serrated saw blade bit into his fatty upper arm under superhuman force from Nora, and the numbing tourniquet was pale substitute for general anesthetic or surgically tied blood vessels. Jove hollered, grabbed desperately at Nora's wrist, but she wanted him with reciprocal fervor then. And she would not be denied. Turned out, Jove was a screamer. Nora thrusted and thrusted and thrusted thrice more before releasing him howling from the prison of his left arm.

Jove shivered and shrieked up to sitting, unable to take his eyes from the blood-pouring, expertly crafted wound at his shoulder. Only the steely grip of Nora's unfaltering fingers around his throat halted his cries, and, then, he heard her voice again, up from the floor.

"It was you. All along, it was you."

Jove regretted his momentary resistance. Nora held him as he wanted for so long. She stopped his screams and soothed his pain. She forgave him in his darkest moment. And she did not let go.

Alabama Nightmares

7

Huggin' Molly

The mud poured like sands down the necks of a thousand shattered hourglasses. Every drenched grain bullied away precious atoms of oxygen fallen into the red clay bunker Douglas and his friends scooped out of the Abbeville clay with hands and feet and Big Gulp cups for two days straight. Only one of those feet remained in the collapsed pit then, a filthy boy's size 10 Buster Brown peeked out where Enos Walker slid down into the makeshift fort but a few seconds before and set off that burnt orange avalanche. Douglas pulled at his hair with cruddy hands, turned silently to Rueben, who dropped to a knee in stunned protest of the reality of what just happened, and then to Gretchen, who already leapt at the dirt pile ahead of her frightened calls of Enos' name. Her velocity pulled Douglas and Reuben into her wake, and she slammed cupped hands into the soft mush on landing. Douglas grabbed the foot, and it ripped away, just a shoe empty of the pale, sockless appendage that normally called it home.

Enos was buried under there, about four feet down, with no air, no light, and no way out. His three best friends dug away milk quarts of heavy dirt in two-handed load after two-handed load, but the forces of gravity and adhesion were stronger than any collection of eleven-year-old hands tired at twilight on that hot July Sunday in 1983. Their channels to where Enos might lay filled in again as fast as they opened them. Enos could hold his breath longer than any of his compatriots, and he proved it on the regular when Gretchen's mama drove them up the road to Blue Springs in Clio. But his record was about two minutes and thirty seconds, and they dug for twice that before realizing they were outmatched.

"We gotta get help," Douglas admitted between gasping inhales, "It's almost dark, and he's been under there too long."

Without acknowledging him, Gretchen kept clawing at the endless pit. Reuben cried, stopped, then slammed his fists into the mud.

"He's dead!" Reuben yelled, "He's dead. We're all dead! The sun's going down, and Molly will get us before we get help!"

Gretchen stopped at that mention, threw a dirt clod hard into Reuben's chest.

"Huggin' Molly ain't real, Reuben!" she bellowed, "What's real is we gotta get Enos out from under this mess and now!"

"She is real," Reuben retorted, "And she ain't gettin' me!"

He darted from the fallen clay fortress and did not look back on his trajectory toward the horse trail that led back to Field Road and, about a mile on, to Douglas' house. Every pore on his body ionized in fear, Douglas shrugged earnestly at Gretchen and took off behind Reuben. The wind whistled past his famously protruding ears as he flew. He imagined himself The Flash, a crackling red streak of heroism en route to pass up Reuben and save the day himself. A stifled cry behind him interrupted his jagged sprint. He approached the already stopped Reuben while he turned to look back for Gretchen.

"Was that Gretchen? Where is she?" he asked, probing the dimming trail behind him through squinted eyes.

Reuben's brown-black irises surrendered to the intrusive whites of his eyes, and he pointed to a black mass between them and Enos' burial site. Somebody was there. A rotund grown-up faced away beneath a veiled funeral hat and hovered over the buckled white legs of Gretchen. Its heavy black robe writhed and wriggled in silent work, interrupted only by skinny white arms stretched partially around its bulk in taut embrace.

"Huggin' Molly!" Reuben screamed as if calling to the thing, "We're late getting home!"

And he rabbited toward the road again. Douglas procrastinated a moment, still uncertain he saw what he saw, but, then, she looked at him. The pallid fat face rotated from the flaccid figure of Gretchen to smile at him across the thirty or so yards that parted them. The glinting pupils screamed, "You're late!" The harm embedded in that steely telepathy propelled him behind and swiftly past Reuben, cloaked again in his Flash fantasy. The familiar tumble of elbows and knees behind him presaged the cry of a fallen kid.

"Ungh! Dougie, wait!" Reuben yelled as he went down.

Douglas slowed to sub-sonic speed to look back one last time. Reuben lay crumpled on the grass, tried to collect himself, and stared pleadingly at him. Before even his reflexes allowed action, the burgeoning evening coalesced its dark rays over Reuben, wove Molly's cloak from matter in that void of the light. The rest of twilight's enforcer materialized within the black of that garment. Hands that pulled Reuben from the ground to her bulging bosom. Blistered lips that whispered inaudibly in his ear and blanked his eyes and his will with their unknown telling. Arms that wrapped about the boy's little frame. And Reuben's limbs reciprocated as she issued her quiet reprimand for staying out too late. The loss of a friend was no excuse!

Reuben's hug accomplished, another little body dropped from the dark of Molly's robes. It was Gretchen, her expression drawn into a fright mask as though frozen in funny face play, as foretold by all mothers everywhere since the beginning of time. Her hands clenched in contractures of shock. Her body tied in a faux rigor mortis from her minutes in the wafting hell of a place within Huggin' Molly.

Reuben was Molly's then, too, and Douglas was even later getting home. It was either the front door or the hug for him, and he would not end this day smothered like Enos and Gretchen and Reuben. The darkening world about him crawled to slow motion. He pantomimed stretching The Flash's cowl over his eyes and nose, and he was off with gritted teeth, the ground aflame at each touch of his hyperkinetic feet.

The sun cowered beneath the tree line opposite Field Road as Douglas turned to ride the white line on the asphalt that led to his driveway. The night dropped around him, and all the imagined speed force his mind could muster was unlikely to get him home before Huggin' Molly did to him what she'd already done to his friends without super-speed. He fought the urge to look back, focused on running. His lungs burned. His throat hurt. His legs wanted to quit, but he just had to gut it out a few more minutes, and her claim to him would be voided with but a touch of the screen door handle.

If only speed were a factor…

The dark thickened about him, smoke black and cold and reeking of mothballs. The coalescing cloud moved with him, zigs or zags or feinted stops or starts, until the fabric of Molly's garments flailed about his face and arms, and the world outside it vanished. The sleeves and collars roiled like eels in a drought-bled creek and smelled worse. Douglas slowed before they tripped him. He tried to stop, drop, and roll, as if the blackness was fire, but the crepe-skinned arms that grew in the robes held him up. The collar unfurled in a vomit of varicose, cadaverous flesh to unveil Molly's grinning countenance. Her sunken charcoal eyes sparked beneath the hat that wove itself from strands of greasy gray hair.

The race home was lost, and Douglas knew he deserved what he was about to get. He stiffened in wait for those waxen old arms to encircle him, thought of all the times Mama warned him about getting home before the streetlights came on. He never minded her, so he would pay the price. The hug didn't come immediately, though. Molly still held another to be released before Douglas took his place between clasped fingers and chest.

Reuben, his face stretched and frozen in a death grimace like Gretchen's, was birthed from Molly's night clothes. He melted through her release and into the world outside, fallen to their joint decision to defy twilight's simple curfew. And it was all Douglas' fault. The dirt fort was his idea. Finishing it at the cost of staying out too late was his idea, too. Like Gretchen, he didn't believe in Huggin' Molly, and Molly knew it. The fact of his skepticism was the source of the gleeful glimmer in her eyes as she took him into her embrace. He felt the justice with every cold breath on his ear when she squeezed him to her, and she began her whispers.

They were low mumbles at first, incrementally rising in volume and pitch with each utterance. All the wind left in Douglas escaped in that hug, replaced with the Arctic gales piercing his ears then in thunderous screams of rebuke.

"Honor thy father and thy mother!"

"Do as you're told!"

"Stop running in and out!"

"Don't you back-talk me!"

"You'll do it and like it!"

"You better get home before dark!"

A rapid-fire medley of each and every parental warning ever imagined, and all of them stampeded through Douglas' formative little conscience like a herd of blazing bison. The realization of his guilt in all aspects pulled at his heart and at his face with forces beyond the physical. His eyes burned with tears that did not come. His mouth curled and spasmed with cries silent from empty lungs.

Was that what Enos felt in the belly of the fallen fortress? A fear forged in helplessness from his own defiance of the most basic parental cautions? An acceptance of the ultimate price paid for a prize so stupid?

Enos lay face down and drowned in red clay, lost and alone with no friends left to tell his folks what happened. At least Douglas had someone to hug.

Alabama Nightmares

8

Midnight Madness

Friday night at The Galleria was Times Square on New Year's Eve juxtaposed on middle Alabama. Wrap in a circle of suburban vampires and poverty-level ghouls who too worshipped at the temple of Bauhaus, and Nixon was truly home. His black-clad pack of horror fiends prowled the dead ends and empty spaces of the mall like vengeful haunts tied there by the unspeakable acts that killed them. Waves of dead-eyed wives in mom jeans steered their crotch goblins away from the assembled coven upon rounding a corner into their trench coated midst. A quick line from *Return of the Living Dead* or *The Lost Boys* always sent the little conformists scurrying back to the bright-lit safety of Montgomery Ward.

"Brains! Live Brains!' Nixon blurted at a rotund, feather-haired blonde and her brace-faced tween as they dared emerge from B. Dalton Booksellers. The pair actually flinched at his panto-mimed zombie lurch, and his jet-dyed friends howled.

"Go back to Sinatra, Mama," Jenice spat at the family in passing. Her sarcastic head jerk pulled her asymmetrical bangs from the glittering green eye usually obscured behind them.

Nixon's face tightened at the look of her. She was every leathery fantasy born of late nights soaking in the videos of MTV's *120 Minutes*. Pale, gaunt perfection in combat boots. And she left him the note, the one asking him to stay after the mall closed… to spend some alone time.

Or at least he thought the note was from her. It was Magic Marker scrawls folded into a paper football and stuffed in the inner left pocket of his coat, the one so sacred to house his first Skinny Puppy cassette.

"Aladdin's Castle after hours," it read.

Nixon reflexively patted the bulge in the fabric, confirmed note and tape still hid together there, checked his watch face beneath its Wite-Out-lined anarchy symbol. 8:37 p.m. Time to disappear until security kicked all the sheep out into the night, locked up, and went home to cry into their checkbooks.

He pulled the corners of his trench coat into his most daunting Bela Lugosi Dracula spread, drawled, "And the hour draws nigh, my coven, for me to make my escape."

He eyed Jenice, eager for smiling acknowledgement. She bit into her gum and flipped him off with a smirk. Yes. YES. No more words needed speaking. Nixon low-fived tall Cory and split the crew like the Red Sea en route to his premeditated hideaway.

The arcade was just four stores down, on one of the short corridors onto the second-floor parking deck. He floated in with ten minutes to spare and slid a quarter into Hyper Dyne Side Arms. A few moments of side-scrolling ultra-violence later, and Todd, the attendant on duty, clapped his shoulder in an unspoken *wrap it up* and made his nightly jaunt to The Great American Cookie Company next door to flirt with the little redhead with the pixie cut. Clockwork.

Nixon released the joystick mid-barrage to violate the sacred space of the Employees Only doorway to the office and stock room of Aladdin's Castle. Adjacent the emergency exit was an empty Q*bert cabinet forgotten there to the annals of video game evolution. He dropped to a squat and slid serpentine between wall and wood into the voided dark and waited.

The clink of the dropped and locked gate signaled Todd's return and heralded the stark silence of some fifty games going black at once. Eager slurps of snogging replaced klaxons and whistles and trespassed uncomfortably close. Todd was more persuasive than Nixon guessed. The office make-out session was brief, as the two came to a quick decision to move the festivities to her mom's Grand Prix.

The door closed behind them and pulled Nixon from the rising dark as though coalesced from the very shadows. The upper right button on his watch shown a light onto its hands. 9:22 p.m. The guards usually left early, but not before 9:30. He dropped into the ragged office chair, put his feet up, arms behind his head. And he waited.

Nixon woke with a start and almost threw himself from the chair. The chirps and strobes of the arcade machines blurred from the dream they'd just interrupted, and, for scant seconds, he didn't know the where or the when of his existence. But his watch anchored him to 11:02 p.m. at Aladdin's Castle. Damn it! Jenice was gone. He passed out, punked out, and missed her.

He wobbled to his feet, kicked the rolling chair into the wall in self-disgust. The throbbing pulse in his forehead pushed his eyes from the cascading kaleidoscope of the game room, but something moved in the periphery. He squinted into the beeping spectrum interrupted by a petite, feminine silhouette.

"Jenice?" he whispered beneath the gurgling electronic cacophony.

Nixon shielded his tender vision with a forearm and lumbered into the nearest row of fluttering cabinets. She was gone, but her hum alongside the Donkey Kong theme betrayed her retreat to the opposite corner of the space. He stole a moment to collect himself into the Goth god he became every Friday and Saturday night and slow-mo-turned the corner to face his admirer, but found only the disintegrating skull of Dirk the Daring on the Dragon's Lair screen.

His veneer of cool survived the miss before the spectral peacock's tail of lights that framed him there like the victorious Kurgan from *Highlander*.

"There can be only one," he muttered to his surging courage and turned on a heel past one of two facing Double Dragon games. A few cabinets down, she lingered there, just an absence in the prismatic convulsions of the arcade, propped, chin down, against the console. No, beside…maybe within…the console.

Nixon ignored that trick of the light, smiled his most sinister with a cock of the head.

"I got your note," he half-gloated, instantly embarrassed at the banal wretchedness of his one bad shot at an impression.

And the stupidity of the words set in when she slipped between the machines and out of view. Desperation propelled him to the split past Polybius and before Super Pac-Man, but it was only a couple of inches wide, too small for anyone to…

The Polybius screen pulled his attention to a familiar face that stared back at him there, derezzed and pixelated, but plainly recognizable. It was Jenice, angled bangs and all. That swelling, ascending whistle of B-movie laser beams rang in triplicate as her lips mouthed silent words that instead typed themselves across the glass.

"Thank goodness you're here, NIX."

The sentence faded. Polybius Jenice blinked once.

"I've been waiting for you to save me, NIX."

The face froze and fractured into a swirling vortex of pixels, flushed itself into a black screen of death.

Then, words.

"Player 1 Ready!"

Nixon reflexively grabbed the joystick, rested his left index finger on the action button.

The game set itself up in a reverse regurgitation of the dissolution of Jenice's face moments earlier, and the same mute lips pushed words across the screen.

"Save me, NIX. Save me from Polybius."

And the face dropped to a miniscule, low-resolution version of itself in the center of the display, surrounded then by concentric layers of colored bricks revolving opposite each other. He depressed the action button, and a white pixel mass dropped in from the top of the screen, struck a brick, disintegrated it. His joystick was slaved to a set of four equidistant paddles on the outskirts of the constricting brick walls. He deftly shifted the nearest one to bounce the ball back into the brick, blasting it away like the first.

This was just Arkanoid in reverse, and he *knew* Arkanoid. Less than a minute in, and he shattered a corridor through the brick to

Jenice. When it rotated to grant her little icon horizontal access, all motion stopped, and her digitized head smiled and tumbled end over end through the flashing opening and off-screen.

A quick fade to black preceded the spinning head flying into view from the right edge, as though continuing its motion from its escape. It careened off the left periphery and then back into view from the right on to a crude, digital planet that materialized there. The two collided, but only the planet remained. Words blinked into view.

"And the hour draws night for me to make my escape. Save me, NIX. Bring me back to you."

He did it! Jenice was with him, and she knew he saved her and that he did it right. No teachers to report him. No parents to criticize him. No brothers to out-do him. This win was his, and nobody was taking it from him.

"Player 1 Ready!" Polybius flashed before him.

And NIX took the controls of an obsidian-shelled starfighter, thorn-sharp wingtips and tail grown from a fuselage like the metal body of the blackest bat. He slipped into atmosphere on the trail of Jenice's beacon, blinded by poison vapors, illuminated, for once, by purpose. A tap on the right control primed the machine's teleportation beam as he neared her, saw Jenice standing expectantly on the cratered rock of Polybius, the burning capitol behind her, smirking in all her shimmering leathered finery.

"Engage," he murmured to the ship's computer, and the flash of the teleporting searchlight dropped ship-to-ground like a static vortex and found her, embraced her, brought her aboard, to him. Wordlessly, she dropped into the pilot's seat adjacent and took the reins. Mirrored eyebrows and lips curled as eyes cut each unto the other in knowing swagger, and twin yokes pushed forward into thrust to carry them up and away from this lost and lonely planet.

In the morning, the arcade manager, Todd, poured Visine into sleep-dried sockets before hoisting the Aladdin's Castle gate to prep before open. The unexpected whir and scream of the machines greeted him, and he scanned the space before entering in case an intruder lurked. But it was empty of people. Only one thing was out of place. There, on the floor, was a creased and crumpled flier that read, "Aladdin's Castle after hours." One of about a thousand he stuffed into avoidant hands and unwitting pockets the previous month when The Galleria granted permission for late hours as they debuted their newest game…Polybius.

Alabama Nightmares

9

Bouquet of Blood

A top hat was always a sure symbol of the elite, something true even in those times of famine in the little, lost town of Eclectic. And a top hat was all Catherine saw above the crowd scrambling about the man they all called The Traveler in the cemetery drive that still, hot July evening. Her neighbors said he was all that kept the common folk alive in those days after the crops were razed, dropped from their stalks by the blade of one devil-spawned plowman, if one were to believe such tales. Whatever the truth, Mr. Fairless, owner of every field, delivered no grains, no corn, and no melons to market in Spring. And the people grew desperate.

Catherine squeezed young Samuel's hand in signal to advance with her to the bustling scene before them. Excited, thinning denizens left the throng then, brushed past with corked and blown-glass spheres of liquid in their strained clutches. The Traveler's voice sounded above the din of beggars, as through a tin megaphone.

"Hunger is a body's weakness of need! Starvation is punishment for gluttonous consumption beyond that need," he preached, "I bring elixir to make meat where none remained."

Catherine and her boy stepped through the disintegrating crowd and into view of The Traveler and his cart behind a sickly, pustulous old nag. Beneath the web-strapped stovepipe chapeau, red-orange strings of hair framed a face hidden behind welder's goggles and a two-foot leather proboscis that masked his nose and mouth like an aardvark. A half cape of rags complimented an angled kilt of the same over leathered pigskin the length of arms and legs. And, on his back, a steaming translucent tank tubed to the facemask and filled of the same green splash seen in every townsperson's new decanter. Circuses didn't tout freaks of that ilk.

The glinting goggles turned to Catherine as she hesitated on approach.

"Step up with that morsel, mother," it gestured toward the staring Samuel, "You want elixir to put some meat on that boy?"

She didn't understand, so didn't reach for the proffered bauble.

"We drink it, and it fills us like food?" she managed.

"You give it to your stock, and they grow muscle and bone and marrow to feed you," The Traveler explained.

She didn't own cattle or nary a lonesome goat, and neither did anybody else in Eclectic without the surname, Fairless.

She countered, "But we...I...don't have any stock."

Another voice, this one warm and familiar rang out behind her.

"Yes, you do, child. We all do. You flaunt yours before us even now," said Father Duncan, and he sauntered toward them, fingertips pressed together in arrogant prayer hands.

The priest stood out among his flock, still thick and strong amidst the poor-bodied hungry and their sunken eyes. That dichotomy scared her more than did the gothic-costumed Traveler, and she pulled Sammy protectively to her thigh, angled her body between him and them.

Father Duncan strode to the side of his supplier and continued, "The good book says, 'Behold, children are a heritage from the Lord, the fruit of the womb, a reward,' and, in times of need, we must partake of that fruit."

The Traveler leaned into Catherine's personal space, handlessly lifted his rubbery snout, said, "And I bring the waters of the Lord to grow that fruit bigger and fuller of flesh to sustain you."

"Mama," Samuel started. He was smart enough to interpret their grave metaphors.

"Don't you fret, Sammy," she reassured him, "We're going home."

"Not empty-handed, you won't," spat Father Duncan, and he produced a pink-tinged package wrapped in butcher paper.

Catherine retreated from the hidden meat as though it was a grenade, tucking Samuel behind her.

"Father, I…I can't accept that," she blurted as he advanced, undeterred by her skepticism.

"Call it the charity of the flock, Cathy. I know you and the boy haven't eaten. Take it," he urged.

The Traveler towered tacitly over that dialogue and dance, a single flask of elixir in cupped hands. Catherine glanced uncertainly at him, back at the priest's incongruent smile of beneficence.

The meat hung in the air between them as if dropped among wolves in winter. The entire scene stilled for moments. Samuel, rail-thin and hopeful, peeked around his mother's hip, caught her guilty gaze as she worried between dealing with those devils and depriving her son again.

Duncan rattled the paper with an impatient shake that betrayed his stretched smile. Catherine snatched it to her bosom, retreated as if she stole it, but The Traveler spoke before she could run.

"You abscond with but a treatment for your pangs, when you might escape with the cure."

He dangled the elixir before him, a bulbous ornament on his tree of lies, and continued his pitch.

"Feed the boy with this meat, and he wants for more in hours, days. Infuse the boy with this elixir, and neither wants for more for forever."

Her eyes scattered among the two entreating her, Catherine blindly disrobed the flesh in her palms.

"What is it?" she asked ahead of the tears to come. Samuel already grasped at it. She heard his lips smack with salivating desire.

Father Duncan dipped his chin, chuckled.

"Come, Cathy. Ask yourself why you question the gracious bounty of our Lord in the very face of His blessings."

"Mama, I'll drink it. I'm hungry," Samuel whimpered, snatched at the red mass in the paper nest in her hands.

His reckless meat lust outran her reflex to avoid it, and he pulled away into his reaching lips a rare plug of fibrous tissue, blood and all. Stubby fingers followed to poke in straying strands and droplets. Fear for her child blended with jealousy and a momentary guess at the taste of those fingers to paralyze Catherine. She noticed too late The Traveler's advance on her boy.

He pulled at Samuel's hair like a handle to open his grinding teeth like some king's grizzly stein and pour in the elixir from its former home. The little tongue flailed desirously about his meal to lap at the chemical waterfall gifted by the fright-masked swindler.

"See how the innocent young decide so simply to treat themselves? Adult wisdom is too often its own curse, Madame," The Traveler admonished her.

Already, a new scent replaced the fragrant hair and familiar breath of this son at her side for eight years then. It was meat, fresh and savory. Not the morsels wending their way down his gullet. His meat. The muscles of his cheeks and neck and forearms swelled and pulsed and, with every minute motion, flicked delicious pheromones into her airspace.

Mute by the horror of her own impulse, she dabbed at the corner of his mouth to clean it, lifted the blood and spit to her own waiting tongue. It was sweet in that way the test bite first off the grill was sweet, and she wanted more. She pushed on Samuel's shoulders to gently seat him in the graveyard dirt, then dropped the remains of Father Duncan's butchery into his lap. She could no longer discern if her delight at the spectacle of his rabid consumption was a result of the satisfaction of feeding her child or of the promise of continued blood zest. She was at once terrified and exhilarated at the play of her senses and drives.

Father Duncan grasped her shoulder, pulled her from those kaleidoscopic emotions, and she realized the reconvened crowd about them. Every eye and mouth beheld Samuel with the same ravenous fervor raging within her. His every bite drew the circle tighter until they pressed into her. The Traveler carved a narrow channel of fear amidst the gathered, backing easily to his cart and horse, his handiwork complete.

The raw, unprepared stench of the starving masses forced the aromatic vapors from Catherine's nostrils, and that angered her. They wanted what was hers, whether by virtue of birth or preparation, and that would not stand.

"Stop!" she screamed at them, but their compounded, malnourished murmurs drowned the word in their currents.

None of them, even Father Duncan then, noticed her anymore. They smelled only the boy meat she spawned, then the epicenter of their picnic. But that was hers to keep, more for possession than for love, but hers, nonetheless. Ahead of her, The Traveler mounted his diseased horse, glanced back to boast his treachery with but a gaze across the cartload of elixir bottles, whose contents gifted that delectable savor to Samuel and might do the same for her. And she was bigger and better marbled than her calf, a choicer cut to draw away the assembled diners and spare her little chunk.

Catherine released a wolfen howl and rushed the rolling cart, The Traveler's lazy trot too slow to evade her suicide mission. She leapt high and cannonballed into the pile of glass balls, exploding shards and elixir and her own sliced flesh in a dispersing bouquet that reached like the hand of a ghoul for the already onrushing commoners come cannibals.

The hormones and nutrients and enzymes invaded Catherine through wounds and orifices and pores, and her muscles and her glands and her skin flourished into a succulent cornucopia laid ready on the floor of the cart as a pig fresh from the spit. And the people of Eclectic wanted her and would have her, and they passed over her tiny treat still stuffing himself back in the cemetery to receive her.

Alabama Nightmares

10

Mudridin'

The local dirt pit swirled with globes and streams of light woven about the undulating chords of Hank Williams, Jr.'s *Whiskey Bent & Hell Bound*. The song of backwoods indulgence was the chosen anthem of Chunchula, Alabama, and it rang out above the grinding engine noises of the assembled pick-ups, Jeeps, and El Caminos scattered within those red clay walls. The hoods and the beds and the open doors spilled over with bored teens taught by honkytonk parents that the one and only cure for workday monotony was found in a cardboard suitcase from the gas station.

Rawley Stevens entered the redneck thunderdome riding shotgun to his cousin, Ricky, the latter a creekside Casanova, if ever one walked those woods. One of the notches on his belt belonged to his 10th grade English teacher, and he could prove it. Rawley, though, was a different animal. The tall, lanky bookworm wished to be paging through his well-thumbed *Monster Manual* before diving into the new *Uncanny X-Men* annual that dim Fall evening in 1987, but the teenage thrum of lust called him away to the only place he knew yielded girls, regardless the true fact that he bore no concept of what to do with them when he found them. Rawley hated beer and whiskey and what they did to the adults who made some effort to raise him down there in the sticks, but his loins and his leanings overtook his ideals on occasion, and that night was one.

Ricky slid his white and blue Z-28 Camaro between two jacked up four-wheel drive car crushers, gunned the V-8 within to herald his arrival, and slid up and through the open window in practiced gymnastics sure to be the utter envy of Mary Lou Retton and Bo Duke, alike.

"Who invited all you sumbitches out to my dirt pit?" he yelled at the pot-bellied offensive linemen and sons of iron workers arrayed about him.

Rawley tensed. Every sweat-beaded brow turned to them, beer can hands frozen apart from lips in the moment. Then, in harmonic unison, they laughed, all of them as they converged on Ricky and his ride, throwing high-fives and howling war whoops through spittle of Budweiser and Milwaukee's Best. If this was country-style Camelot, then Ricky was Arthur and every third girl in the pit a one-shot Guinevere.

Rawley couldn't exit the car. The overbig, beer-bodied high schoolers leaned about the car, and the door wouldn't budge. They didn't notice him, anyway, and Ricky forgot him for the first three pairs of well-rounded, faux-distressed Jordache acid-wash jeans that sashayed past. The car cab rocked and rolled like a kids' amusement park ride, pushed by the butts and backs and feet of Chunchula's best and brightest. Rawley clenched his eyes in self-loathing. That was not his world. Why in Hell did he do this to himself?

After a half-hour of listening to Bubba-bravado and hamfisted sexual harassment, the car-sitters moved away in a herd, their attention no doubt pulled away by some shiny bauble filled with stench-ridden swill. When they lumbered out of sight, confident that none of them would see him get out of the car, Rawley pulled at the door handle, winced at the click of the mechanism as it opened. They could not know he was in there that whole time. He kept his profile low as he slithered from the seat, not letting the door latch fully as he pushed it to. The plan was to just walk home, to weave between the parked assortment of vehicles like a ninja and disappear into the night beyond. He took three steps beneath one of the elevated trucks adjacent the Z-28.

"Rawley!" someone called to him from the direction of the herd, "Hey, Rawley, c'mon!"

It was Ricky. Goddammit. The always grinning, good-looking oaf half-jogged at him.

"C'mon, man. Toby's taking his Dad's Toyota into the mud. I'm shotgun, and you're in the back."

Rawley still faced away from Ricky, every muscle taut, eyes burning.

"In the back, like in the bed of the truck?" he managed.

Ricky clapped him on the shoulder. He was a good dude, despite his predilections for alcohol and dirt road pussy. Getting Rawley in the bed of that truck was Ricky's idea of a favor, and if he wussed out then, it was he who would be the pussy.

"Yeah, dumbass, the bed of the damn truck," Ricky guffawed.

Rawley pulled a smile across his lips and turned without lifting his toes from the clay.

"Cool, let's do this," he said.

Taking the first ride into the mud was some kind of local honor bestowed on only the most promiscuous stud and his chosen court, and Rawley walked the red dirt carpet adjacent his preening cousin like they were Charlie Sheen and Emilio Estevez at the world's worst awards show. At the end of the jeering gauntlet waited a jacked up, candy-apple red Toyota SR5 Xtra Cab, custom painted and raised to accommodate tires to dwarf most tractors thereabouts. A gleaming black roll bar stood like a gate to the underworld behind the cab and would be Rawley's best friend for the next twenty minutes.

All of a sudden, he couldn't breathe. Why did he do this to himself?

He clambered into the truck bed without hesitation or a glance at the drunken throngs and instantaneously dropped himself before the right leg of the roll bar. The low thrum of the engine lent a foreboding vibration to the rippled black plastic liner, and Rawley cringed with every change in its frequency, in dread of the acceleration to come. A minute or two passed without movement, and he opened his eyes to verify they were still, realized he was not alone back there.

Clamped onto the opposite leg of the roll bar was a girl from his Algebra class. Jennifer was her name, or maybe Jessica. Concentration sucked when he was scared. She smiled at him from a softly tilted head.

"Hey, you're Rollie, right?" she asked. She was pretty, with eyes so brown they were black and a bleached white-girl perm, and she was chubby in that alluring way country girls were chubby, all round hips and tits and lips. Her button-flies strained to keep everything hidden where it needed to be. Rawley forgot his predicament for a precious moment.

"Rawley, yeah," he reminded, "Hey, Jessica."

"Jennifer," she laughed, "Everybody does that."

"Sorry, I…"

The rev of the Toyota's engine cut short Rawley's intended apology, and the truck lurched forward to lift the front tires. He wrapped his arms around the roll bar and his eyelids around his pupils as though thrown from a plane. Jennifer laughed some more.

"You gonna be okay back here?" she prodded.

"Y-yeah, just wasn't expecting that," he uttered between pallid, fake-smiling lips.

A warning rang from the cab. It was Ricky, drunker and louder than just minutes before.

"Y'all hold on back there! We about to flip this mug!"

And they were off, spinning clay into the crowd through to the dirt pit entrance and into the dark. The truck fish-tailed in the muck, the bed swinging wildly side to side in sudden acceleration. Rawley and Jennifer bounced hard against the bottom and walls of the bed liner. She squealed and hollered with glee. He made no sounds other than the impact of his limbs on the hard plastic. How in the world was this fun?

A hard, leaning left into the trees, and they hit the good mud, so thick and stanky even the dark couldn't hide it. The stuff filled every tread of the tires and every void of the wheels, but the lowest of five gears would not be denied. All four wheels spun in the mire, the forward pair throwing the gray muck into the bed, pelting Rawley and Jennifer with stinging clods of the shit. When the tires all caught traction at once, the whole truck moved, and Toby upshifted and hauled ass, fish-tailing again to the point the bed sideswiped a tree on Jennifer's side. He did not slow down, instead glided forward preternaturally over the mud's surface with tires spinning at a high rate out of synch with the slower velocity of the entire vehicle. It was that sweet spot in the ride, when the bumping and swaying stopped, and country boys walked on dirty water for the promise of feminine spoils to come.

Rawley relaxed for a second, made eye contact with Jennifer, who then appeared as done with the ride as he was from the start. He smiled, and she softened in return and smiled back. She was pretty.

Ricky yelled something from the cab, and the truck swerved left. The bed spun in the mud all the way to the front of the trajectory. Rawley screamed. Jennifer screamed. And the Toyota twisted heavy into an old oak, the cab slamming sideways on the trunk. Its momentum flipped the chassis rightward and flung Jennifer and Rawley clear and down a hidden embankment.

Rawley woke to an acrid smell. His left nostril filled with mud, but his right detected gasoline on the air. Dad was burning limbs again. He tried to sit up, but his back hurt. A lot. There was smoke from the bank above him. Dad? Were they camping on Chickasabogue to run trout lines? God, he hurt. He twisted his back to try to stretch the pain out, and his repositioned ears caught low grunts from up top, like a hungry horse face down in a feedbag. But why would horses be out...he froze.

A bloodied and contorted girl lay facedown in the creek, not ten feet from him. Arms and legs weren't supposed to bend those ways. The truck. *That GODDAMN TRUCK.* Why did he agree to ride? Why in Hell did he do this to himself?

Rawley reflexively crabwalked back from Jennifer's body. Yeah, Jennifer. She liked him. He could tell, and, then, she was dead. *Dead because of MUD RIDING.* Needless and stupid and dead.

A shadow in his periphery pulled his eyes up, and he was not alone. A man, a big one, stood up there where the smoke and gas billowed and looked silently down on him, scanned the creekside scene until his gaze fell on Jennifer. He grunted that horse-snorting grunt, and another guy, with the same massive build and long, tousled hair, appeared next to him. A body hung limp over his shoulder. They said nothing, just lingered there taking in the situation and grunting as though expunging the thickest of phlegm from their throats. After a moment, Rawley smelled them, their rancid scent that of a wet dog doused in vomit. He gagged, tried to turn away from the stench, heard the wet impact of the man's body on the mud as he did so. Splatter caught the back of his neck and his hair, the sensation jerking him back the other way to see what fell.

It was Ricky. One remaining eye stared into oblivion, his jaw unhinged below the left ear and hanging from shredded flesh at the right. His arms fell unnaturally from dislocated joints, and a leg was missing entirely, though Rawley couldn't tell which from the tangle of humanity before him. The tingle of fear invaded his disorientation for but a moment when the things were upon him. They moved silently, so much so he didn't notice them descend the embankment, one to hoist Jennifer into its molting, orang-utan-haired arms and the other to corner him between water and bank and its 8-foot height and 9-foot wingspan. Knots and dreads of matted black fur clung to the creatures' every square inch. Glistening, obsidian eyes and a wet nose emerged over a minor snout of gnarled fangs and teeth that emitted grunts louder and lower than before.

Rawley tried to crabwalk again, his legs too afraid to carry him any other way, but the beast punted him into the stream with a swift right kick to the abdomen, right where he hurt so bad. All breath left him, and he landed hard on the rocks in the shallow brook. He expected it to pounce on him, but the assault did not come.

From the woods above rang the grinding engine sounds of the other kids from the dirt pit. Strobing beams of headlights pierced the black up there, and the monsters – that's what they were – were gone. And so was Jennifer. Rawley pulled himself up to kneel in the creek, even as Southern accents thick as the mud yelled in the distance for Ricky and Toby. He formed a distress call in his throat, but it never escaped.

A big paw grabbed his ankle with crushing strength and yanked, effortlessly pitching him forward, face first into the drink. But, where…

He bounced out of the water with a busted forehead and bloody mouth and tried to find the subduer still latched on to his leg. The grasping forearm led into the empty creek current, as if the waters themselves reached out to hold him, and, then, it yanked again, pulling him below the surface and a good twenty feet upstream in one jerk. Amidst the chaos of the violence, he felt kicking feet swimming beside him in the depth of less than two feet. His face and head ricocheted along the rocky bottom for a minute, maybe more, before the motion stopped.

Rawley bled and hurt and spun dizzy, tried to catch a breath. He floated in a still, little pond that stank of algae and dead fish. The impulse to sit statue-like to avoid detection won out, and he waited for something to happen. The plop of the interrupted pond surface caused him to start and to gasp. He looked to the sound to find Jennifer's corpse erupted from below to float adjacent him, followed instantaneously by the dog-and-vomit odor of the things.

The first sat up from the water with no sound whatsoever, the filthy runoff silently returning to its source. The giant body unfolded from legs to shoulders like a spring-driven child's toy to glare down on Rawley. His senses flared, and he rolled eyes and neck rightward to find the other one soundlessly behind him. The aggressive grunts reignited, and Rawley clenched his eyelids, grew angry with himself again.

Why didn't he just stay home? Why in Hell did he do this to himself?

Each of the shaggy beasts grasped at his limbs, his wrist and elbow secured by one and ankles by its accomplice, and they tore him apart from each side of himself with a fervor no different, really, than the torture of choice he had inflicted on himself every moment of his existence.

About the Author

A lifelong resident of coastal Alabama and a career mental health practitioner and executive by trade, Kevin LaPorte realized his aspirations of writing fiction in the arena of comics in mid-life, beginning self-publication of a line of horror comics with partner, artist Amanda Rachels, in 2010. After dabbling in prose for the first time since high school, he felt inspired during the pandemic years of 2020-21 and got serious about it. *Baptizer and 10 More Alabama Nightmares* is the culmination of a teenager's dream atop the foundation of a seasoned, self-published writer's fiction acumen, and it's just the start for Kevin in the world of prose. Thank you for being here.

Engage with Kevin on Substack at:

kevinlaporte.substack.com